Doctor March looked up at his daughter.

"Of late you haven't been yourself," he said. "How long is this nonsense to continue? I talked to Nellie Grand this morning. According to Nellie, you're just a nurse going through the motions of being a nurse."

"If she's dissatisfied," Dawn interrupted her father, "let her hire someone else."

"She could do that, too," said Dr. March. "You're lucky to work under Nellie. You'll learn more with her in a year than you'll learn in five years with anyone else."

But Dawn March didn't realize how much she had to learn. Not only from the strict, yet compassionate, Nellie Grand, but from Dan Colby, the gifted painter who chose to make his living selling junk; from Dr. Ken Jones whom she wanted to marry, and even from Mrs. Clara Royce, her rival for Ken's affection. In fact, it was through Clara Royce that Dawn learned the most important lesson of all!

● ● ●

AVON BOOK DIVISION
The Hearst Corporation
572 Madison Avenue—New York 22, N. Y.

NURSE MARCH

•

WILLIAM NEUBAUER

NURSE
MARCH

DAWN CLOSED THE REDWOOD GATE BEHIND HER AND ambled up the street to do battle once again with Wes Overton. Mrs. Elliott spotted her, of course, and hailed. Mrs. Elliott then pushed up from her knees and came briskly to the fence for a chat. "Girl," she reproved, "your Pa had to do his own driving."

"Hi, Mrs. Elliott."

"Good morning, Dawn. Don't you know that your Pa's much too nervous?"

"Or bad-tempered?"

"Some men can drive," said Mrs. Elliott, "and some men can't. And suppose Dr. March had an accident? Who'd deliver my granddaughter's baby, eh?"

"There are other doctors."

"If you ask me, Dawn, some girls ought to feel ashamed. While they humor themselves, nice men like Dr. March and Wes Overton get nothing but work and bad treatment and—"

"Just the same, Mrs. Elliott—"

"Nice girls don't interrupt their elders. Do you know what I think is wrong with you? You're getting very peculiar with the spring. You take a good dose of sulphur and molasses, and maybe Dr. March and Wes Overton will get the nice treatment they deserve."

Dawn waited, a grin quirking her lips and twinkles lively in her deep brown eyes.

Mrs. Elliott grimaced. "No," she said, "I don't have a single question. Knowing you so well, I know you wouldn't discuss a former patient anyway."

"That's one of the rules of the profession, Mrs. Elliott. Need anything at the store? Or postage stamps, perhaps?"

Mrs. Elliott lifted her gaze skyward. She was a small, frail-looking woman with prominent cheekbones and alert, very clear gray eyes. She was approaching her seventy-third birthday, but her carriage and complexion belied the fact. Her

7

sudden laughter did, too, coming quick and fresh from her throat with the happy-go-lucky quality typical of the laughter of the young.

"Not," she said, "that I wouldn't love to hear all about it. Such a scandal! And such a tremendous sum of money! Only what did he do with it? According to the paper this morning—"

"Exaggerated, I'm sure."

That, it developed, was a blunder. Now the gaze of Mrs. Elliott came down from the cloud-speckled, blue April sky. "Girl," she said, "what an interesting opinion. Just wait until I tell Mr. King!"

Dawn winced. She turned and started to leave, but wisely changed her mind. Give Mrs. Elliott the chance and she was certain to tell everyone in town that the former Dover nurse was a hundred percent convinced that Mr. Dover was absolutely innocent! Then calls from the bank and calls from the district attorney's office, calls from her boss and goodness knew who else. A very clever woman, Mrs. Elliott. Give her the chance to wag her tongue and she'd defeat you every time.

"Look," Dawn said, "I didn't exactly express an opinion, ma'am. I was actually discussing newspaper headlines in general. You know how they tend to—"

"Shall we have coffee, dear? I'm sure you must want some coffee. Oh, I know you young girls. You simply refuse to eat proper meals and sleep proper hours. Dash here, dash there, hurt this young man, hurt that young man, call the district attorney a liar, call the newspapers liars, and go careering on your way straight to a nervous breakdown."

Mrs. Elliott shook her lovely white head.

"I'm very glad," she announced, "that I had my youth when the young could enjoy their youth."

And Mrs. Elliott opened her picket gate, and gestured.

Feeling annoyed, yet amused, Dawn followed her across the yard and up the steps of the board-and-batten house. She made a discovery up on the porch. Mrs. Elliott, she saw, had made a fine beginning in her latest spring clean-up and spruce-up campaign. The boards of the front wall were a bright, brave red and the battens were a crisp, fresh white. The front door, too, had been newly and expertly painted, and only a hyper-critical eye would have noticed that certain of the doorpanes had been reddened, as well.

"Like it, dear?"

Dawn said from the heart: "You sometimes shame me."

Mrs. Elliott looked over the white picket side-fence at the yellow cement-block home of Dr. March. "Well," she said consolingly, "Wes Overton will be handy around the house. He's a very bright and industrious young man. I'm sure he'll do the jobs that are practically screaming to be done."

"Oh, am I to marry Wes?"

Mrs. Elliott opened the front door gingerly. "Now mind the paint, there's a dear. It would be such a shame to ruin that pretty skirt."

"Glory, ma'am, you're in fine form this morning, aren't you?"

"May I ask you a question, dear?"

"Well?"

"Don't you feel dreadfully undressed in those—well, those drawers?"

"Bermuda shorts, Mrs. Elliott, aren't drawers."

Mrs. Elliott gave her customary sniff, then skittered on before Dawn to the kitchen. In the kitchen doorway she said startlingly: "Wes, dear, please cover your eyes. Some women dress, some don't, and your young lady happens to be one of the latter."

Dawn whirled, but never made it. Wes came out of the kitchen quickly. His hand stabbed out, got her wrist, held on tightly. "You know what?" he asked happily. "This meeting must have been destined."

"Let me go!"

Wes let her go.

He moved around her, however, to block the way to the front door. "Surprised to see you up," he said conversationally. "I telephoned Nellie, and she told me you were on a rough case."

Dawn did the only thing possible with becoming, if self-conscious grace. She walked on into the kitchen, her brunette head high, her slim figure ramrod straight. She took a seat at the yellow dinette table and methodically lifted the coffee pot and poured herself a cup of coffee. She deliberately ignored the curious eyes. She sipped the coffee, decided it was strong enough, and sipped again.

"Wes painted the front of my house yesterday afternoon, dear. Wasn't that nice of Wes?"

9

From the Elliott porch, Dawn thought, a jealous fellow in love could keep a good eye on the March redwood gate. He could see fellows come and go, if there were fellows to see, and he could also keep well-posted on the comings and the goings of Miss Dawn March. Fine! Only then what? And what a sad waste of time!

She looked up as Wes took the chair opposite her. She said carefully, "Nice of you to help Mrs. Elliott. And you helped me, really, because I promised to do the painting for her."

The kitchen door was closed. A moment or so, and the front door was closed, too. There was a sudden silence that was so deep it got on Dawn's nerves and she had to say, for the sake of saying something: "You did a very nice job, too, Wes. Only how can you afford to take the time from your work?"

Wes drew a deep breath, a big man, his eyes reddish-brown, his curly brown hair lustrous in a pale beam of sunlight. He was good-looking in his rugged fashion, although he wasn't cleanly shaved and his hair had encroached upon the rightful territory of his ears and neck. He finally said, as if the words didn't much matter: "I like the old girl, and I like to help people I like."

Dawn's nerves relaxed. There was little to fear, she knew now. When Wes could sit before her and speak so calmly he was manageable. It wouldn't be much of a battle, after all. Probably she could settle the matter in five or ten minutes, then get back to the house to finish her uniforms.

"And how's Ken?" Wes asked. "We were supposed to go bowling last night, but he begged off at the last minute. Said he wasn't feeling too well."

"Oh?"

Now Wes smiled gently. "Ken and I have a great deal in common, haven't we? Or perhaps not. I doubt he could possibly love you as I do. I have fewer distractions, among other things."

"Or just haven't fully matured?"

Wes laughed.

Dawn took another sip of Mrs. Elliott's coffee. She felt a pang of hunger, and glanced around for something to eat. It wasn't necessary, however, for her to go to the exertion of getting bread from the breadbox and butter from the refrigerator. Wes did the honors, moving with an interesting grace for so big a man. He dropped two slices of whole wheat bread into the Proctor toaster and depressed the switch. "You should eat more," he said. "When you were a kid you had a fine rolypoly figure, and I approved."

"Wes!"

He was pleased to reminisce. He said softly, almost in dreaming tones, "Those were the good years, Dawn, did you know? You had time for everything. Remember how we used to go to the beach to watch the sea lions? And do you remember that time I rented a boat with an outboard motor and took you halfway to Anacapa Island? You never did want to go home, as I remember."

Remembering more, Dawn flushed. That was the afternoon Wes had become aware of her as a girl, and after that everything had changed. Strange, how a mere peck on the cheek could destroy a good friendship. Why hadn't she laughed? If she'd just laughed that afternoon Wes might have laughed back and the whole thing might have died then and there. Instead . . .

"Ah, well," Wes said, "you're not difficult to look at now. No dinner, no dance?"

Dawn's brown brows drew together. "Are you psychic?"

"Your father gave me the news. Big speech by the great Dr. March, so a mere mortal like me will have to change his plans."

That offended Dawn. Her flush deepened, and sparks gleamed in her deep brown eyes.

"The trouble with you," Wes said, "is that you don't even know a tyrant when you live with one. And even if you did know he was a tyrant, you wouldn't care. Behold the nurse, behold the doctor, and that says it all, doesn't it?"

The toast popped up and temporarily distracted him. He buttered a piece for her, a piece for himself. He served her, and reached for the coffee pot. "What you ought to do," he then went on, "is marry me while you still have something to offer."

"Now there's a dear proposal, Wes!"

"I ought to break a leg. That would interest you, wouldn't it?"

Dawn chuckled.

And Wes glumly pushed on with the familiar words that seemed to make sense to him even if they didn't to her. "Your tragedy, Dawn, is that you've been trained to think of human beings as sick bodies poised between life and death. You can't recognize a well human being as a human being. Do you know what?"

"Isn't Ken well?"

It was as if she'd not spoken.

"Hang it," Wes asked, "what's wrong with being an average woman and seeing an average man as he is, and succumbing to an average woman's instinctual longing for a husband and children? Hang it, why do you always have to be such a dedicated nurse and doormat daughter?"

Dawn blinked. Now this, she thought, was a different approach. And it wasn't an amusing approach, either. Hadn't Ken himself told her just last week that she was far too engrossed in her career? Good Lord, had the two fellows gotten their heads together?

Wes stood up, shrugged. "Well, that's the end of the lecture for today. What about dinner and dancing tomorrow night?"

"Ken wouldn't like it."

"You're not engaged. I doubt you'll ever be engaged. Sure, he likes you. But Ken likes many people."

That stung. Dawn resented the innuendo, and lashed back. "Anyway," she snapped, "I've outgrown you. Wes, you idiot, time moves on and people move on, and you either have to move on and grow with people or—well, just look at you! Suppose I were in love with you? Suppose I had that instinctual longing you mentioned? What would it amount to? What could it amount to?"

"I make a buck."

"But oh, no, there you are just plodding along as you've done all your life."

"My own man, at least!"

"And you'll just be plodding along when you're sixty."

"And still be courting the spinster, do you think?"

That did it. More disturbed than she wanted Wes to see, Dawn got up hotly and headed for the service porch door. "At least I'll be eating!" she snapped. "And I'll be doing a few things, too."

12

She clattered down the service porch steps and hurried across Mrs. Elliott's back yard to the white picket gate in the side fence. She found her father sitting in the patio, a cigar between his teeth, his gray head exposed to the sunlight. He gave her a hearty wave and zestfully pulled a scrap of notepaper from his jacket pocket. "Wondered where you were. You recall how the lecture died just after the subject of obesity? Well, I think I found a fine transitional paragraph."

"Good for you."

"Just take a chair, young lady, and listen to your father spout."

It seemed to Dawn that somewhere in the distance she could hear Wes Overton laugh. She ground her teeth, shook her head. "Things to do, Pop. And would you like to hear something interesting? According to Wes Overton, I'm doomed to be a spinster because you and Mom have trained me to see human beings only as sick bodies poised between life and death."

Dr. March crinkled his forehead. "When did he learn to spout such words?"

"And you, Pop, happen to be a tyrant."

Dr. March chuckled, a rather small round man with a cherubic pink face and twinkling blue eyes. "I did my best," he bragged. "If you're not a crackerjack nurse, blame your mother. At the wrong times, I'm sorry to say, your mother made me spare the whip."

"I'm a crackerjack nurse. In fact, I'm one of the most competent visiting nurses in the county."

"Beauty is becoming, wit is becoming, virtue is becoming, but neither smugness nor complacency is becoming."

Dawn continued across the patio. Her destination was the small ornamental pool her mother had recently had built as the first step in her program to turn the March patio into something that would resemble a formal Japanese garden. "A fact is a fact," she said coolly. "And I'm not quoting my own thoughts; I'm quoting Nellie Grand."

Her father was visibly astonished. "Miss Grand actually told you that?"

The compliment had been earned, Dawn thought. In that wretched hovel in the Mexican quarter of Oxton last week she'd earned Nellie's compliment.

"You neglected," Dr. March said testily, "to answer my question."

"Pop, didn't Ken telephone?"

He scratched the side of his nose. He was obviously tempted to fib, but to his credit he finally nodded. "A few minutes ago," he said dourly.

Dawn's eyes came alive. She whirled, her young figure tense, her roundish, dimpled face almost embarrassingly hopeful. Standing there thus, she troubled Dr. March. So young, so quick and warm with life, so eager for the unknown, so vulnerable.

"I was quite annoyed with Ken," he said candidly. "He had quite forgotten that I am scheduled to lecture at Town Hall tonight. He had the effrontery, too, when I told him, to suggest I could do my own driving. As if I would be in a fit condition to drive."

"What was the message, Pop?"

"Some nonsense involving dinner at his home. I of course informed him that would be utterly impossible. Now, then, shall I read you that transitional paragraph?"

"You did *what?*"

Dr. Roger March stood up. Perhaps five feet five, he seemed to her almost six feet tall in his indignation. "Surely," he demanded, "I have the right to expect you to drive me to that lecture?"

It hit Dawn then that Wes, in his way, had been right. No, her Pop wasn't deliberately, cold-bloodedly a tyrant. But in his self-centered, good-humored, bumbling sort of way . . .

She drew a sharp breath and made her decision. "I'm sorry you told Ken that," she said quietly. "This is pretty important to me, Pop. Or do you want me to end up a spinster?"

"Did you actually take that Wes Overton pup seriously?"

Dawn didn't answer, saw no reason to. Her heart thumping, she dashed back into the house. So he had called after all? He'd remembered, as men in love were supposed to remember such days. In the living-room she loosed a happy sigh. "Ma," she said, "I've been a goop."

Chapter II

At SIX-FORTY-FIVE EXACTLY DAWN ALIGHTED FROM HER Plymouth sedan before the Jones house in Maricopa Street. She shivered in the cool ocean wind. The booming surf drew her gaze to the ocean, and for a moment the magnificence of the rolling deep and sharply delineated islands held her breathless. This, she thought, was a sunset. How many shades of red were there, and how many shades of blue?

A gate creaked open, clicked shut. Harriette Jones chuckled and asked: "Care to buy our house, Dawn? For a mere fifty thousand it's yours."

Dawn whirled, looked, was disappointed.

Again, Harriette Jones chuckled. "Nope," she said, "he hasn't come home yet. He's doing a tough job at the hospital, or so he said."

Dawn turned back to the view of the ocean. It was difficult to conceal her disappointment, but she somehow managed it. "I do love your view," she said. "But only on clear days and nights. And you don't have clear days and nights very often, do you?"

"What about forty thousand, if it's a cash deal?"

The wind strengthened appreciably. Sand came blowing in from the beach to pepper their faces. Dawn grabbed at her hair, then had to grab her skirt, too. Harriette noticed, of course, and frankly laughed. "That'll teach you to make a social event of an invitation to dine with the Jones folks. Glory, what are you dressed for—romance?"

Dawn headed for the house. She supposed it wasn't good etiquette to beat her hostess into the house, but she didn't care. She took off her coat in the small vestibule and carefully hung it on the steel gray costumer. She examined her hair in the full-length mirror affixed to the turquoise wall. A few curls out of place, but it didn't matter. And it wouldn't matter, would it, if the wind and sand had played havoc with her tan cashmere dress? Just another dinner with the Jones

15

folks! Dressed for romance? What a howler! She stabbed an angry glace at the pebbled glass door on her left. She wished Ken were inside, sitting in his dental chair. Just give her a minute or so with one of his fiendish drills and perhaps . . .

"Sherry, Dawn?"

"No, thanks."

"Well, I'm having one. To celebrate. Just think, a year ago you and I were strangers. Now here we are, practically friends!"

Uttered as Harriette had uttered it, the comment was heart-warming. The girl wasn't a person who liked people at once or who gave her friendship easily or indiscriminately. Touched, Dawn changed her mind. "To that I'll sip, Hattie. What time do you expect Ken?"

The question wasn't answered at once. Harriette led her into the living-room, a quick, slim, very attractive blonde creature with a lilt in her every step. A lamp was turned on behind the spice brown sofa, and another lamp was turned on across the room.

"Do you like nuts and raisins with your sherry?" Harriette asked. She gestured at a frame portrait-photograph on the mantel-shelf of the brick fireplace. "My grandmother taught me to munch nuts and raisins while I was sipping sherry. A very nice grandmother, Dawn. Some of the happiest days of my life were spent in her old house in Salem. You'd have loved her, I'm sure."

"Nuts and raisins, of course."

Harriette went out to the kitchen for the sherry. She was gone perhaps five minutes, and during that time the wind strengthened and the boom of the surf grew louder. The sounds were company for a moment, and then they took on a quality that was depressing. Feeling alone and lonely, Dawn looked around for something to read or do. A fine beginning, she thought, for an anniversary celebration. Not, of course, that Ken should be here with her rather than where he was. A dentist, like a doctor or a nurse, had to do his job when he received a call, because if he were "out" or otherwise unavailable some poor human in pain would continue to experience that pain. Still, it was odd that Ken hadn't telephoned her to explain.

Harriette came in with a silver serving tray held high. A bottle of sherry and two glasses and a cut-glass bowl heaped

16

with raisins and nuts gleamed as she crossed the room. "Anyway," Harriette grinned, "this will give me the chance to ask some questions about the Dover family. Weren't you startled when you heard of his arrest?"

"Very much so."

Harriette poured the sherry. She gave her guest first crack at the raisins and nuts, as a good hostess should, then went over to her favorite channel-back chair near the fireplace. "I wonder what ever prompted him to steal all that money, Dawn."

Dawn shook her head. She said from the heart, "I doubt I'll ever understand it. I worked as his wife's nurse for several months, you know. That was last year, just before you people came to Port West. Mrs. Dover's left kidney had been removed, and there were certain complications. For perhaps two weeks after she'd come home from the hospital she was in a highly critical condition. Actually, my Dad didn't expect her to live. Ever lived or worked in a house where someone is terribly ill, perhaps dying?"

The blonde head shook from side to side. A whistle came into the wind, and somewhere a shutter or a loose door or a loose gate banged, and then the surf boomed like a thunderclap and the banging sound was engulfed.

"There's tension," Dawn said quietly. Her brown eyes were narrowed and thoughtful now, and the set of her jaw was grim. "You say to a worried husband that there's little to fear, that his wife will recover, but he knows in his heart that you're only mouthing bromides to cheer him up. He waylays you in the hall. He just happens to come out to the kitchen while you're brewing yourself a cup of coffee. And his face is so pale, there's such agony in his eyes, and his hands are trembling so badly . . . well, that's how it is when a woman someone loves is terribly ill, and perhaps dying."

Harriette Jones betrayed her age, her inexperience. She gave a melodramatic shudder. Thinly, she giggled. "Dawn," she pleaded, "will you stop talking that way? Why, it gives me the creeps."

Dawn shrugged. "The point is, Hattie, that Mr. Dover was one of the most attentive husbands a dreadfully ill woman ever had. And he was one of the kindest, most considerate employers I've ever had. I don't know why, but it's difficult

17

for me to believe that such a man could—well, abscond with money as they say he did."

Dawn sipped the sherry, and found it tasty. She took another sip, then filled her mouth with several crisp cashews and a half-dozen raisins. While she was chewing the nuts and raisins the door chimes rang mellowly.

The woman, whoever it was, refused to take no for an answer. She was very firm with Harriette out in the small vestibule. "I think," she said firmly, "that Dr. Jones will want to see me, Miss Jones. He is, after all, my dentist."

"But—"

"My dear child, am I to stand in this bitter-cold vestibule and freeze?"

Harriette wasn't ever given the opportunity to answer that question. Heels clicked on the hardwood floor; then a tall, beautiful woman with glossy black hair and deep blue eyes made a graceful entrance into the living-room. She saw Dawn, gave a smile, then sat down on the sofa and casually crossed her legs. "I'm Clara Royce," she introduced herself. "If you've never patronized Dr. Jones before, I can assure you his work is practically painless." She looked left as Harriette came in, and quirked her thin, arched brows. "Now, now," she said soothingly, "I have no intention of taking your brother out for the evening. This is actually a visit of a patient to her dentist."

Dawn, startled, took a good long look at Harriette's face. She didn't like what she saw in the girl's large gray eyes. There was a certain fear in those eyes, and something more, something she couldn't quite define. But what in the world?

"Dawn March," Harriette said, "may I present Mrs. Clara Royce? Mrs. Royce owns several farms over toward Oxton and is spending a couple of months in Port West."

"How do you do," Dawn said.

Mrs. Royce unbuttoned her simple black coat. She was wearing, it developed, a Davidow suit that almost exactly matched the color of her eyes. It also developed that Mrs. Royce owned a striking figure of which she was justifiably proud.

"Dawn March?" she asked. "I believe I've heard of you, Miss March. Your father is a doctor, is he not?"

"Just the finest surgeon in all California, that's all," Harriette asserted.

18

Mrs. Royce smiled at this gaucherie. "Well, dear," she said, "I'll give him my patronage should I ever require important surgery."

"And Dawn," Harriette said, more tautly than ever, "just happens to be engaged to my brother, that's all."

There was silence except for the eternal boom of the surf and the continued howling of the wind. Dawn, embarrassed, didn't know how to break that silence, and Mrs. Royce, incredibly, seemed quite content to have it go on and on and on.

Harriette returned to her chair, picked up her glass of sherry. "I was just drinking a toast in honor of the engagement, Mrs. Royce. Care to join me?"

"Is it domestic sherry?"

"California sherry."

"Thank you, no. I find California sherry unfit to drink. It lacks, shall we say, distinction."

"Do you like anything in California?" Harriette asked. She stood up, seemingly on the verge of an explosion. Dawn got up, too, her brown eyes smilingly apologetic.

"I think," she told Mrs. Royce, "that now isn't the time to badger Harriette. And as for Ken . . . he only works evenings when it's an emergency. You're obviously in no distress, and so . . ."

"My dear Miss March—"

And that was when Ken Jones came home from a trying hour at Port West Hospital. The usual bounce was lacking in his step. He trudged in as a farmer might trudge in after a long, long day of irrigating his crops. He nodded left and right, but never stopped en route to his green leather chair. Dropping into the chair, he said: "Good strong coffee, Sis, there's a dear. And lace it with cognac, will you?"

Dawn tactfully went out to the kitchen with Harriette and volunteered her services as a coffee brewer par excellence.

Harriette inhaled deeply. "Well," she said dolefully, "you may as well hear the rest. You and I are the unwanted ones, not Mrs. Royce. She needs to see the dentist, my eye! She's here to find out what's what because I telephoned you this morning instead of her. Darn it, Dawn, I'm sorry."

"You telephoned? But according to my father . . ."

"Well, you were supposed to think Ken had remembered.

19

And if he had the brains of a gnat he would've remembered, too."

A lump formed in Dawn's throat.

She had a strange sensation of being cold, freezing cold, and yet at the same time she felt so warm, so choked for air, it was all she could do to remain there and allow the windows to remain closed.

Chapter III

NELLIE GRAND SAID: "FOR SHAME!" AND KEN AGREED. Nellie Grand added: "She's too nice a woman, Ken," and Ken agreed with that sentiment, too. But it seemed to Ken Jones that the opinions of Nellie Grand were of no importance. And it further seemed to Ken Jones that the niceness of Dawn March was of no importance, either. Clara Royce was the woman for him. But how to arrange a marriage, eh? How to convince her that he, Ken Jones, was as vital to her happiness as good health, good clothes, expensive jewels?

"Young man," Nellie snapped, "you're wool-gathering."

Ken gave her a quizzical glance, and grinned. "Stop scolding me, Nellie. I'm not one of your pauper patients who has to endure your incessant nagging."

"Are you bereft of your reason, young man?"

"I think not. I certainly hope not."

"Who is this Mrs. Royce? Obviously, she's a divorced woman. She's obviously a clever woman, too, because she seemingly is well-supplied with money."

"And she's quite beautiful, too, Nellie. She has what I like to term electric presence. The instant she entered my office a month ago I was—"

"For shame!"

"For shame."

"Actually," Nellie confessed, "I'll be quite content if you never see Dawn again. A very competent, dedicated nurse. Give her five years, at the most, and she will be well qualified to function as my staff assistant."

"Nellie," Ken grinned, "I'll nobly sacrifice my interests to further the career of that competent and dedicated woman."

The sharp brown eyes of Nellie Grand appraised his face. They approved it, from broad, unwrinkled brow to square-cut chin complete with cleft. In fact, Nellie thought it was a most prepossessing face, and when you added the figure of Ken Jones to it and threw in that mane of gilded hair for good measure, it was decidedly a face with a future.

"Ken," she said, with noticeably less asperity, "allow an older woman to give you the advice your mother would give you if that dear woman were alive."

"That dear woman, as you call her, was an unholy terror, Nellie, and I'll thank you not to mention her again."

And, abruptly, it wasn't a prepossessing face across the table from Nellie in the Oxton Hospital café. The little woman gave a cluck, shook her head. "I accede to your wishes, young man. Nevertheless, I shall give my advice. I suspect you have little to offer anyone except your face. You're an indifferent dentist. Indeed, I'm quite astonished you received your license to practice in California. In short, you have no asset worth mentioning except your face. So do it justice, young man; use it well."

His jaw muscles tightened.

Nellie Grand was unperturbed. She leaned forward, clasped her hands on the table and asked: "Now, then, have you carefully looked into the matter of her finances? It would be regrettable, Ken, if some fine day you were to discover you'd not married as well as you could have. I insist that a searching examination be made of her financial position."

He laughed, thinking that comical. And then a certain stillness of her eyes, a certain quality of pity in the set of her mouth, brought him up hard and short. He said huskily, "You're a most peculiar woman, Nellie. A very peculiar woman."

Their conversation was disrupted at that point by a young woman, shabbily dressed, who took a seat at their corner table. The woman looked glumly at Nellie Grand. "Well, I did what you said, and then the hospital did what I predicted."

Nellie smiled coolly. "Perhaps the social worker knows a bit more about her business than you do, Kathleen. Now stop pouting. No one intends to take your child from you. It's simply a question of providing the child with the food and medical care he requires."

"Sure, Miss Grand, sure. Big-hearted folks, all right. But do any of them offer me a job so I can give the kid the chow he needs?"

"Are you qualified to hold a job?"

"I can do something. You bet I can do something!"

"Or, Kathleen, you can attend business school and learn to do something more than low-paid work. Now you get out to my car and wait for me. I have no intention of letting you down, and that's a promise."

The woman sat there, thinking it over. Ken and Nellie Grand waited, Ken lighting a cigarette, Nellie composedly sipping her luncheon coffee. Finally the woman nodded and hurried between the rows of white-clothed tables to the street door.

Ken blew a puff of smoke over the iron-gray head of Nellie Grand. He smiled wryly. "You have your hands full, don't you, trying to help this person and that. Well, I'd better not detain you, Nellie. Anything more to say?"

"One thing more, young man. Do you have the slightest concept of what you're doing, where you're going?"

He stood up, very well dressed and groomed, and very assured. "I believe so, Nellie. Don't bother about the bill—I'll pay as I leave."

As he left, too, Nellie Grand was exasperated almost to the point of tears. There was a young man, she was convinced, who badly needed to be taught a good lesson!

A few minutes later, out in her car, Nellie disposed of the Kathleen Wyman problem. She wrote the woman a check for a hundred and fifty dollars. She thrust it into Kathleen's strangely reluctant hand. "You will take this," she ordered crisply, "and go to Miss Lorello's secretarial school on Avenue C. You enroll for her full course of instruction and you will dutifully attend every class and you will dutifully practice your typing and stenotyping. As for your living expenses, I shall discuss your problem with a very generous family and arrange for them to mail you a small check weekly. There. By the time your child has been discharged from the hospital you'll be gainfully employed and you'll both enjoy happier lives."

Kathleen swallowed. Her eyes round, she sat staring at Nellie Grand's face. Another moment or so, and there'd be tears!

Nellie asked quickly: "Kathleen, why do you suppose Dawn March has such difficulty holding a man?"

"Miss March?"

Nellie nodded, hoping the device would work.

It worked. Kathleen knit her forehead and did some serious thinking. Instantly, her eyes cleared and the threat of tears disappeared. "Ah," she said, "I don't know, Miss Grand. It could be lots of things, like her Pa being such a big shot in Port West, or like she makes it pretty darned clear she cares a lot more about her work than for most people."

"And yet, Kathleen, she does care for people. I shall be quite frank with you, because I'm interested in having your opinion. At one time I doubted that Dawn was seriously interested in people. I thought she'd simply drifted into nursing because it would please her father and perhaps satisfy her yearning for a . . . well, a certain drama. So, of course, I deliberately assigned her difficult but undramatic cases in some of our more ghastly slums. She never complained, nor did she ever fail to do a good day's work. I think, therefore, that she cares for people."

"As folks who need help, maybe. But you know what I think, Miss Grand? I think that when folks are just folks to her, then they're just folks, see, and nothing more!"

The thought disturbed Nellie. Her mind worked busily on the matter throughout her drive back to the county seat of Santa Anastasia. In her offices in the small visiting nurses' building in Cherton Way, she made a sudden decision. To her secretary she snapped: "I'm changing Dawn's district, Berry. She'll be assigned the Port West-Oxton area from the ocean to Oxton Road. You'll switch Sandy to Dawn's old district, and you'll switch Helene to Sandy's old district. Understood?"

Mrs. Berry glanced up from her typewriter. "Certainly, Miss Grand. The Health Commissioner telephoned while you were out. He wanted to ask a favor."

"I never do favors, Berry. I thought you understood that."

"He hoped you wouldn't mind transferring Dawn March to the Port West-Oxton district, Miss Grand."

There were times, and this was one, when Nellie Grand wished there were something she could do about Berry. Berry had been with her too long. Berry needed to work in another office where some intelligent and heavy-handed supervisor would slap her down whenever she presumed to play games.

"You might have told me when I came in, Berry."

"You were so engrossed in thought, Miss Grand."

"Nevertheless . . ."

"And shall I be frank, Miss Grand? You don't handle the Commissioner too well. You snap. You refuse to tell him

24

practically anything he wants to know about the work of the association. That's all right, of course, under ordinary circumstances. But the Commissioner is a politician, a man who has to be elected every four years. Such a man has to know something about the departments, agencies and the like under his supervision."

"Forget my order, Berry. In due time I shall make the transfer, but not now."

Mrs. Berry nodded dubiously, as if to say it was Miss Grand's affair, of course, but that she personally didn't approve of going out of one's way to offend the Commissioner. And the attitude of Mrs. Berry troubled Nellie Grand throughout the rest of the day. Berry knew her job, all right, and Berry knew the political world of Santa Anastasia County and the city of Santa Anastasia, too.

Frowning, Nellie Grand tilted back in her swivel desk chair and stared thoughtfully at the opposite office wall.

Again, she made a sudden decision. She picked up her telephone handset and proceeded to dial the Health Commissioner's office. The Health Commissioner's secretary was sarcastic.

"Oh, certainly," the secretary said. "And I'm the queen of Oshkosh."

"I shall wait precisely ten seconds, young lady. At the end of that time I shall break this connection and be out to see Mr. Struther."

Between Nellie's ear and the secretary's ear the telephone connection hummed.

Then, less sarcastically: "Is this really you, Miss Grand?"

Nellie testily held her tongue.

A job being a job, the secretary took no risk. "Well, Miss Grand, I'll just tell Mr. Struther you said you were you. All right?"

A moment later the voice of Commissioner Struther came booming against Nellie's eardrum.

"Nellie," he boomed, "good to hear from you. How's the finest nurse in California, Nellie, eh?"

"Quite well, Commissioner. And you?"

"Couldn't be better, Nellie. Nellie, did you get my message?"

"I received your message, sir."

"Now, Nellie," he said forcefully, "I'll fight to the death

anyone who presumes to interfere with your splendid management of the affairs of the visiting nurses' association. Under you, this civic and county agency has become a splendid weapon against disease, human suffering, and even death. Is that quite clear, Nellie?"

"What is your interest in Dawn March, sir?"

"A fine girl, Nellie. The fine daughter of a fine doctor and noble friend."

"I see, sir."

"Not that I approve of her infatuation for Ken Jones, Nellie. I don't. Still, it seems to me that a girl who gives so much of herself to the community should certainly be given every reasonable opportunity to see the man she mistakenly loves."

Nellie barely suppressed a giggle.

"Furthermore," said Commissioner Struther, "her father has implied that he would appreciate this consideration."

Nellie drew a deep breath. An interesting development! Did the girl's mother know?

"Well, sir," she said noncommittally, "I shall consider the matter very seriously. It isn't my custom, as you know, to shift the girls from district to district. Patients develop confidence in and respect for the girls who come faithfully to their homes week after week, month after month. It is always very difficult for patients to adjust themselves to—"

"Nellie, I thank you. I have always held, Nellie, that you're an entirely reasonable woman."

"Oh, and while we're talking, Mr. Struther, have you authorized a certain renovation I requested?"

"Please," he begged, "don't be unreasonable, Nellie. I do my best with my limited budget."

After hanging up Nellie pressed her buzzer, and when Mrs. Berry stepped in Nellie dolefully ordered: "Make the transfers after all, Berry. It will be a dreadful waste of good nursing material, but there it is. Oh, and will you get into touch with a painter and have him do something about our walls?"

Mrs. Berry met the eyes of Nellie Grand, and smiled.

"I've already typed up the transfer order," she announced. "All you have to do, Miss Grand, is sign it."

Nellie Grand grimaced and fidgeted, but finally, of course, she signed the transfer.

26

It was luck as much as Dawn's own powers of observation that told her she was being followed. She was stepping from the Heiser Stationery Store on Oxton Plaza in Oxton when a squealing kid in the middle of the park attracted her attention. The kid was just squealing in indignation because a pigeon was keeping well beyond a pair of questing hands. Dawn laughed, but as she swung her gaze away from the kid she noticed Wes sitting on a bench under one of the Plaza's towering palm trees. Wes loafing at this hour of the business day? Dawn compressed her lips. She got into her Plymouth sedan and drove on to her next call over in Port West. It was no trick at all to pick up Wes Overton's gaudy Ford sedan in her rear-vision mirror two minutes later.

At that hour of the overcast April morning there were few cars on the road and very few people to see. It was possible to work as a girl drove along, and Dawn worked. Mr. Dan Colby. What manner of person was he? He obviously needed the services of a visiting nurse, because Nellie wasn't the sort of woman who assigned a nurse to a case before she'd conducted an investigation to determine that the need for a nurse was urgent. But a broken leg? Clearly Mr. Dan Colby wouldn't perish of his broken leg, so why assign a registered nurse to him? It was quite peculiar.

And another peculiar fact was that Nellie Grand had given her little briefing. That was so unlike the woman it was almost incredible. Nellie was such a stickler for routine, such a staunch advocate of what she was pleased to term method. It was almost a law in that grubby building in Santa Anastasia that a nurse always discussed a new case at length and in great detail with Nellie Grand. But this morning Nellie had simply handed her the name, the address, the medical report and said: "Drop in to see this fellow today, March. Know him?"

"No."

"Well, it's a rather sad case. You might spend two hours with him today just to become acquainted with him."

"And perhaps tomorrow you'll transfer me to some other district?"

"March, don't be sassy. Where is your sense of discipline? Or are you cross because there was little work to do in your old district?"

"That isn't true!"

"I shall expect a written report this evening, March. Now you'd better be on your way. I have several important appointments."

Dawn had to smile at her memory of the conversation. Miss Nellie Grand, she perceived now, was adept in the art of changing the subject. A quick attack to evade answering a difficult question, and the revolt crushed before it could even be begun. Some day, she thought wistfully, she'd like to be a Nellie Grand. How convenient always to keep your wits about you, always to keep a good five yards ahead of the opposition, always to control a situation and so come out the winner. Too bad she'd not kept her wits about her last week. How utterly routed she'd been. And why? Because she, of all persons, had been confused, then panicked, by a few words spoken by a man too tired to know what he was saying or doing. Had she just kept her wits . . .

She stopped for the traffic light on Port West Avenue. She remembered that she had a follower and she quickly stuck her head out the window to smile at Wes in the gaudy Ford sedan. But now it was too late for Wes to be embarrassed. It was quite in order for him to be in his car in that vicinity at that hour of the day. After all, a real-estate broker had to get around.

"Hi," he called, "want an early lunch?"

"Business."

"Want an early dinner?"

"Business."

He wasn't to be discouraged. "Well, what about chow sometime, somewhere, some year?"

There was no need to answer the question. A truck behind Wes swung out around him, and the driver of the truck beeped his horn. Dawn hurriedly shifted gears and drove on swinging left into Florence Road a couple of blocks south, and angling off southeast toward the city dump and the ocean.

Now the scenery changed. This was the section of Port West the Port West Chamber of Commerce never mentioned in its publicity folders detailing the numerous merits of "the seacoast town with a big future." In this quarter of the town, the past had not yet caught up to the present. The houses lining Florence Road were cramped, weather-beaten, decrepit. Their fronts were dingy with the dust that passing cars kicked up from the unpaved roads, while their weather sides were fuzzy with peeling paint and pockmarked by patches of sand. Few yards bore looking at twice. Most were eyesores compounded of old boards, old discarded furniture, scraps of metal reddish-brown with rust, and all were whitish with blown beach sand and sprinkled patchily with beach apples. The yards, for some reason, were more depressing than the houses. She supposed that was because no one expected much of anything terribly old and terribly worn out. But the yards—well, they seemed to shout that people who lived along Florence Road just didn't care a jot about how they lived or how their children lived, either. Dawn's brow furrowed. Something would have to be done about Florence Road sooner or later. If not for the sake of the adults, then for the sake of the children. Children had to be taught during their formative years that neatness and order and beauty had much to commend them. Otherwise those children would grow up to create several dozen Florence Roads in Port West!

She was happier when she drove beyond the last of the houses. Now the road was heading for the sea, and before her the beach, the ocean, the sky, lay cleanly and beautifully to the eye. She felt tempted to stop her car and go barefooted across the sand to the restless, ever-changing water line. It would be agreeable to sit there alone and think about Ken and herself, the things she should do, the pattern she wanted her life to take. But there, nagging at the back of her mind, was that same deplorable sense of duty that had always kept her moving along and had earned her the reputation, at least in certain quarters, of being a girl dedicated wholeheartedly to her career. She grimaced. Yet she was unable to stop the car. She finished the drive to the city dump, spotted a house of sorts just within the gate, and gloomily got her kit from the floor. Her gray skirt flapping in the breeze, she took a quick look around at the dump, gave a shiver, then headed over the sand to the house. Her first knock was ignored, but her second one was answered. Assuming that the growl was an invitation to enter, she entered. She found Mr. Daniel Colby inching across the floor to let her in.

He smiled easily, pleasantly. "Hi, Miss March. You're early, aren't you?"

"Hi, Dan. Doesn't doing that make you wish you weren't?"

He gave a mock sigh. He stroked his chin like a man wondering if he could do without a shave. "Well," he said patiently, "I resent being bed-ridden. Furthermore, I have the effrontery to doubt that I actually fractured the bone. The doctor who called it a fracture is a quack."

Dawn set her kit on the floor. She gazed around the big room curiously. Except for the bathroom and perhaps a kitchen, she decided, it was a one-room house. And not an unattractive house, either, everything considered. This Mr. Dan Colby, it would appear, had his pride, his self-respect. There'd been no hopeless letting-go here, at least. The furniture was in a good state of repair, the floor was actually clean, and all the windows neatly hung with fresh curtains.

Dan Colby startled her. Seated on the studio couch now, his injured leg stretched out along the cover, he said pleasantly: "You have tact, Miss March. Or was it merely a professional gesture?"

Dawn chuckled. "You seem to have a low opinion of us, Dan. Ah, we aren't so difficult to live with. Simply believe us when we say you have a fractured ankle and we'll get along nicely, you'll see."

"The knee, Miss March, not the ankle."

Dawn bit her nether lip.

He rolled up the right leg of his blue denim trousers, She started, made a quick, worried rush across the big room. She said tensely, "Now that was a foolish thing to do, Dan. How can the bone knit if you remove the splints and—"

He stopped her short by jabbing his forefinger into the puffiness of the right knee. "Doesn't hurt a bit, Miss March. Listen, I'm not entirely an idiot. I have many things to do with my life, and I have no desire to try doing them as a permanent cripple. My knee wasn't fractured. The quack they brought in knew enough not to take chances, I'll give him that much credit. But the knee was never X-rayed. And your Helene Myerson refused to listen, and your Nellie Grand

30

refused to listen, and so I took matters into my own hands. Care to see me lift it and wiggle it around?"

It occurred to Dawn at that point that someone had made a dreadful mistake. She didn't, however, permit Dan Colby to try to prove his point. "Let's assume," she said lightly, "that you have a damaged knee and that you don't want to aggravate the injury. Incidentally, where did you put the splints?"

His black eyebrows arched slightly toward a rather deep furrow that ran along the center of his forehead for perhaps three or four wiggly inches. "Oh, somewhere," he said casually. "What did you want to do with them?"

"Bandage them back into place, Dan. If the doctor thought your knee should be immobilized, then your knee will be immobilized. I'll have one of our county doctors give you an examination, however. Perhaps we'll haul you off to the hospital in Oxton for an X-ray."

He gave the matter serious thought, taking time over it, lighting a cigarette.

Dawn, with a schedule to maintain, decided to hurry the business. She opened her large, heavy kit and took out bandages and a pair of wooden splints. "Well, no matter," she said. "I imagine this may hurt a bit, but it won't kill you."

He yielded with a heartfelt sigh. He reached down under the studio couch and drew out the discarded splints. "Why do doctors and nurses always want their own way?" he asked.

"We like to have our patients recover, Dan. Incidentally, isn't this a lonely existence for you?"

He fell into her little trap. With a certain amusing display of heat, he took up the defense of his way of life and rattled on and on while she proceeded with the business of bandaging the splints onto his right leg. It was, he told her, the only sensible life he'd ever lived. He was his own man. He could, when he wished to do so, spend most of his hours outdoors. Had she ever lived so close to the ocean, in so lonely a quarter of the beach? Well, it was a treat she ought to give herself some day. She'd discover that beauty could be all the company a human being required, and she'd also discover an infinite variety of sea life worth studying and knowing. He spoke of a young sea lion he had met one afternoon while en route to Harper's Point to catch a bass for his dinner. The sea lion had been splashing its way up onto the beach, and apparently had failed to see the fisherman tramping along toward it. The sea lion had been quite surprised, but not particularly afraid. So he'd studied the sea lion while the sea lion had studied him, and it had been a highly interesting half-hour. An experience such as that—well, Dan Colby wanted to know, how could you have such experiences if you lived in the conventional way and spent your day in mundane activity?

Dawn gently ran her fingers along the upper and lower edges of the splints. "Have I drawn the bandages too tight, Dan?"

"If you have, I'll loosen them."

She said flatly, "Not if you expect the continued interest of our association, Dan. Our boss, Miss Grand, firmly believes we should only help people who help themselves."

He glanced down at his leg. The bandages had been very neatly wrapped over the supporting side splints, and the whiteness of the bandages was very crisp against the background of his deeply tanned skin. He touched the little hump made by his puffed knee. "Not too tight," he conceded. "Yours is an interesting profession, Miss March. I think I approve."

Dawn rose from her knees and returned the unused bandages to her kit. This would be one of her easier cases, she reflected, because Dan Colby was one of those self-sufficient human beings who required a minimum of help. She studied the big room to see if there were anything she could do to simplify the life he would lead as a convalescent. "What do you do about meals?" she asked. "I could bring you a hot plate if you need one."

"No problem." He gestured toward one of the windows that looked out on the sprawling community dump. "I know most of the people who come here, and they're quite considerate. If I need help, I just holler.

Dawn went over to the window. She saw a red pick-up truck following one of the sandy roads between piles of smoking litter and discarded remants of automobiles. "How does this work?" she asked. "If people want to dump stuff do they pay you, or what?"

"Hardly. The more so-called junk the better. People also come here, you see, to do some salvaging. Take metal, for example. About every two months a junkdealer in Los Angeles drives up here to remove the metal at so much per pound. That's how I earn my living."

"They pay you for what they want, in other words?"

"In exchange," Dan said, "I run the dump for the city. I burn the combustibles each night, all that. I doubt that you would term it a romantic way of life, but it does have its compensations."

Dawn didn't understand it. He seemed intelligent, and it was apparent that he'd had an adequate education. Yet there he sat looking quite pleased with himself because he'd found a way of life that suited him. She shook her head.

"As you say," she told him, " I wouldn't term it a romantic way of life."

She was about to tell him more, but a car she recognized drove into the dump and eased to a halt a dozen or so feet from the house. Mr. Patton himself got out of the Cadillac and a few moments later gave a lusty knock on the front door. Dan yelled, "Come in!" and Mr. Patton did. His smile broadened when he sawn Dawn. "Now that's fine," he rumbled. "Dawn, this is what I call good, quick service. You tell Nellie Grand I'm pleased with her organization, do you hear?"

Dawn smiled, picked up her kit and slipped the shoulder strap over her shoulder. Slim, quite lovely in her gray uniform, her brown eyes twinkling, she stepped around the hulking Mr. Patton to the door. "Next time we hit you for a contribution," she said, "make it a big one, Mr. Patton, fair enough?"

He followed her outdoors after she'd said her goodbye to Dan Colby. "How is he, Dawn?"

"Obviously his leg wasn't fractured. I'd say he's doing quite well. Why?"

"You couldn't insist, could you, that he agree to move into my house until he's fully recovered?"

"Oh?"

Mr. Patton wagged his iron-gray head. "It's all such a waste, you see. That fellow has it in him to become one of the great artists of his generation. And what does he do? He sits here in the middle of this awful dump and kids himself into thinking he's found a perfect way of life."

Dawn blinked. "You actually think he's that good?"

"That good," he said emphatically. He stood peering off at the ocean for a moment. "Here," he finally said, "let me put it this way. I made a success in the building supply business because I knew what the market would take and I gave the

33

market exactly what it would take. All right. A painting is something you market, too. So when you think you've found somebody who can paint, you get one of his paintings and go to the market with it. And when everyone you talk to says he'd like to buy a few of the artist's things for his magazine or his home or his club, then you know that that artist can get somewhere. Well, that's what I did with one of Dan's paintings of a sea lion, and that's the response I got. You see? Get him out of this hole, put him to work turning out things for the markets that want his stuff, and in ten years he'll be a name."

"Well, why don't you tell him all that, advise him to grab the commissions while he can get them?"

The fleshy face of Mr. Floyd Patton turned red. He lost his temper. "Because," he roared, "that young fellow doesn't know common sense when he hears it!"

Dawn nodded, remembering that Dan had taken his splints off simply because he'd decided, on the basis of no medical knowledge at all, that his leg hadn't been fractured after all. If he'd been wrong . . . She shivered, and got into her car.

"Well," she said easily, "you'll find some way to make him listen to you, Mr. Patton. Incidentally, it's nice of you to take an interest in him."

He grunted. And then he said something that intrigued her. "That young fellow," he said, "is one of the nicest young fellows you'll ever meet, Dawn—and then some." And back he went to the house.

Chapter V

NELLIE GRAND LISTENED, AND WAS PROPERLY CONCERNED. She telephoned the doctor who had diagnosed the Dan Colby injury as a fracture of the knee, and showed even more concern after she'd terminated the conversation. Perhaps five-feet three, and seemingly all bone and skin, Nellie jumped to her feet and went briskly to her office door. "Berry," she snapped, "we shall want an ambulance at once. And will you inform the Oxton Hospital authorities that I am bringing them a patient to be X-rayed?"

Mrs. Berry, as always, kept her wits. "Our budget is pretty low this month, Miss Grand. May I suggest that a portable X-ray unit be taken to the home of the patient?"

"A knee, Berry, is a tricky apparatus. A permanent stiffening of the knee would impair the patient's mobility. I do not concern myself about money, Berry, when I am intent upon sparing a patient a lifetime of impaired mobility."

"Or," Mrs. Berry suggested, "perhaps an appeal to a local doctor would be even more intelligent. That way, there'd be no cost at all."

"Berry!"

"What do you think, Dawn?"

Dawn's lips quivered, but she didn't quite smile. "Why don't you make the appeal?" she in turn suggested. "At the moment, the March family is living in a state of armed truce. I doubt that any appeal I might make would even be heard."

Nellie Grand said, with considerable admiration, "Your father made a fine speech, Dawn. He has a flair, it seems to me, for presenting difficult medical material in a way that is readily understood by the layman. Perhaps he does oversimplify, at times, but at least his audiences understand him. You should have attended the lecture."

"I'm sorry now that I didn't. But as you so often say, aren't we digressing?"

Mrs. Berry pursed her lips. After a few seconds of thought Mrs. Berry said, "Well, I could make the appeal to your father, Dawn. If he turns me down, however . . ."

"In that case, of course, I could invade his den and accuse him of having betrayed the spirit of his profession. You see? I can always whup the old boy when I'm attacking from a position of strength."

Mrs. Berry at once reached for her telephone. She dialed the office number of Dr. Roger March and presently got the ear of the great man himself. She put the matter to him with what Dawn thought was a nice blend of guile and utter helplessness, and Dawn wasn't surprised when her father agreed to examine and X-ray the injured knee for free. He might be a tyrant, in his way, but he was also a kindly guy who'd earned the good reputation he had in Santa Anastasia County. When she drove back to Port West she was in a happier frame of mind. Another good day's work done, and possibly life at home would be somewhat easier and pleasanter. Only one thing more left to do, and perhaps she ought to do that before she went home. Somewhere inside her a nerve tingled sharply, and Dawn grinned. Well, why not? Surely it would please Wes Overton, and possibly it might do her some good, too. In Port West she turned left and took B Street to Central Avenue, where Wes maintained his offices and dreamed his dream of becoming a great real-estate broker one day.

She found him studying a large map of Port West which he'd spread across the table in his pleasantly furnished reception-room. He looked up, grinned, went directly to her and kissed her cheek. "Hi. The uniform is becoming, I'll admit. I prefer the woman, however, to the nurse. Big day?"

Dawn sat down, suddenly realizing that she was tired. "Big day. It isn't very trying work when you know the patients. You can handle them almost effortlessly once you've learned what makes them tick. But when they're all strangers, and the territory is new to you—"

"How come you were assigned this territory? I thought Nellie made it a policy not to assign you nurses to your home territory."

"Pop."

"Oh?"

"He likes Ken, you see. He feels that Ken will amount to something one of these days. And of course they talk the same language. You know, don't you, that a dentist in this state is given medical training?"

Wes looked down at the map. He made an X with his blue pencil to mark the spot he was interested in, then took her by the arm and led her into his inner office. The inner office, too, was pleasantly furnished. It was equipped with a large golden-oak desk, several leather armchairs and golden-oak side-tables; and each wall except the window wall boasted a framed painting of a sea gull. The birds were beautifully done, too, Dawn noticed. In a queer way, they seemed almost alive.

"I see you're doing well," she said. Her brown eyes sparkled. "That's grand, Wes."

"Bought and paid for, too. It isn't necessarily true, you know, that it's either feast or famine in this business. A fellow makes a good steady income if he puts in the hours I do."

He sat down at his desk. This afternoon he was wearing a medium brown tweed jacket and dark brown flannel trousers. His necktie was brown, too, and although Dawn thought this "symphony of brown" a bit studied, she did think that Wes made an impressive figure behind the desk.

"Sometimes," she told him sheepishly, "I lose my temper and make statements I know are untrue. I never have believed that you're lazy, unambitious, stupid—all that."

"Not," he said grimly, "that I intend to devote my life to a frenzied quest for the almighty buck. I think a fellow owes it to himself and to society to do a good hard day's work every work day of the year. But I don't think life should be twisted into a mean grubbing for money. I think a life so twisted is a life without dignity."

His telephone rang, and it was a long conversation. It was a Mr. Bush, it developed, and Mr. Bush was interested in purchasing the Klingley farm if he could obtain it for a reasonable price and on terms. Wes handled the matter quite efficiently. While he talked to Mr. Bush he reached out with his left hand and pulled out one of the drawers of the card-file cabinet on his desk. He quickly found the Klingley card, studied it, then proceeded to give Mr. Bush just sufficient information to interest him. Terms could be arranged, he told Mr. Bush, but why didn't Mr. Bush come in tomorrow sometime and discuss the matter and perhaps drive out to make certain the Klingley farm would satisfy his requirements? This approach apparently suited Mr. Bush, and an appointment was made for ten o'clock the following morning. Wes gave the matter some thought after Mr. Bush had hung up. He then telephoned old Mr. Klingley that he had a possible customer but that the asking price was a bit too high. Perhaps Mr. Klingley would come down, if necessary, a thousand or two? Yes, Wes said, the farm was certainly a beauty, and if Mr. Klingley wanted to hold out for his original asking price then that was that. Still, a sale was a sale, and it was sometimes wiser to take what you could get. After all, how could anyone be certain another person would come along? Would Mr. Klingley give the matter his most serious consideration?

That conversation completed, Wes returned the Klingley card to its proper place in the card-file cabinet and closed the drawer. "You know the Klingley farm, don't you?" he asked. "It seems that Mr. Klingley wants to return to the East. The place is too much for him now, and anyway, he thinks that the day of the small farmer is over. He could be right about that. I see a great many farms as I drive about the county, but most of them are owned by great corporations. Those corporations have the equipment and capital to plant four crops a year on their land. How can a small farmer compete with them?"

Dawn remembered that she'd once spent a full day on the Klingley farm. That had been about fifteen years ago. Mrs. Klingley had advertised for walnut pickers, and several of the kids in her class had decided it would be great fun to earn spending money by picking walnuts. So they'd gone to the Klingley farm, and Mrs. Klingley had grinned and put them to work in one of her walnut tree groves. That had been a hard day of work. Next year, in reply to a letter from Mrs. Klingley, she'd written the woman that she'd already made other arrangements to earn her extra spending money.

"I don't understand why Mr. Klingley feels that way," she told Wes. "They did very well, as I remember it."

"Probably an excuse he's giving himself. People are peculiar in that respect. They seem under the necessity to justify doing whatever it is that they want to do. I've never been able to understand that. It seems to me that a person has an obligation to himself to do whatever will make himself and his loved ones happy."

"But you can go too far, can't you? I know of one young fellow who seems to have gone too far. Wes, have you ever met Dan Colby? He lives over in the community dump. He's such a strange, sad young man."

"Dan? Why do you call him sad?"

Dawn was annoyed with him. "Good heavens, Wes, that isn't the way for any person to live. It's such a—well, a waste!"

"But how could he paint things like that, Dawn, if he were living the usual life in a city?"

Dawn looked at the painting Wes was indicating. In this painting the seagull was hovering just inches from the water, its head and neck describing a small letter "n", its feet outthrust, its wingtips almost brushing the water. It was a beautiful painting in its way, because the artist had somehow caught the wildness and loneliness of the bird, and the wildness and loneliness of the mother sea.

She drew a deep breath. "You know," she said, awed, "that's pretty darn good."

Wes indicated the other paintings. "Some day," he said, "these things will be worth a small fortune. But money aside for the moment, how can you describe such things if you don't see them, and if the description is true, how can you say that he's wasting his life? Do you know the mistake you're making?"

Dawn waited, smiling faintly, rather enjoying this quiet chat with Wes because he was revealing facets of his character and personality he'd never revealed to her before. "Well?"

He leaned forward slightly, and rested his arms on the desk. "You tend to stress the physical, Dawn, That's quite all right. Naturally, as a nurse, as the daughter of a nurse and a doctor, you're inclined to be concerned about physical well-being. But life is also lived inside one's head, and inside one's soul, for that matter. Mental well-being and soul well-being are also vital to a complete, happy life. I think Dan is intelligent to subordinate physical comfort to—"

"But why couldn't he work at a decent job, as others do, and still paint?"

"He told me once that it was largely a question of mood. He goes for a walk. He sees a pelican diving for a sardine. The sight interests him, and he sits down on the sand to watch. Nothing may come of that. Or, on the other hand, there may

39

be something in the sight that strikes a responsive chord in his nature. Who knows what it is? Who knows what makes an artist tick? Anyway, a painting is in him, suddenly, and then it's work, days and weeks of work. That painting you've been admiring . . . it took Dan three months to get that bird exactly as he wanted it."

"And he gave it to you?"

Wes startled her. "Why not? I found him on the beach one day, and we got to talking. You've never been hungry, so it's difficult to tell how I knew that he was hungry. Anyway, I knew that he was, and I took the guy home with me and I got a steak dinner into him, and a few days later I found him a job."

"Wes, how kind!"

The warm glow in her deep brown eyes caused him to flush. He dismissed the kindness with an impatient wave of his hand. "My eye," he growled. "Any person would do a thing like that. Anyway, he didn't like the job and the job didn't like him, and after he'd gone through several unsatisfactory jobs it suddenly dawned on me that he was the sort of guy who needed the outdoors and who needed to be alone. So I heard that Tony was giving up the job at the dump, and I found out that Tony would sell his contract with the city for a thousand in cash, and I got hold of Mr. Patton. You know how nice Mr. Patton is? One thing led to another, and Dan's now at the dump. He gave me these paintings to say thanks."

Dawn almost loved him then. She stood up, grinning. "Why," she teased, "you old softie, you. But don't you know that people who spend their lives helping others are just plain idiots?"

"I don't spend my life doing it," he pointed out. "Incidentally, you may as well answer the question I've been wanting to ask ever since you barged in. How come I'm being honored?"

"I wanted to know something more about Dan."

A flicker of disappointment shadowed the red-brown eyes. Then he got up, too, smiling, a big fellow with an oddly interesting grace. "Any time," he said easily. "What about dinner?"

Dawn gave it thought.

"I think not," she said sadly. "It's been a long hard day.

40

And I think I'm scheduled to do some work on Dad's books."

He took a step closer to her. He asked harshly: "Why do you deny a fellow a chance? What do you know about me, or even think you know? Or what do you know about Ken Jones?"

"Perhaps it doesn't have to be a question of knowledge, Wes. Perhaps you just see a person and that person becomes important to you."

"That's kid talk. That happens, sure, when you're fifteen and lack the ability to see beneath the surface of adolescent emotion. You're not fifteen, you know."

"Twenty-four, in fact."

"And the years going by, years you won't ever get back again. Talk about Dan Colby wasting his life!"

Dawn recognized the signs of an incipient explosion. She thought quickly, and did the only thing possible. She backed out into his reception office and angled toward the door. "Well," she smiled, "perhaps I'm not wasting my life, either. And I won't spat with you, Wes. I think you're a very nice fellow. I think you were kinder to Dan than most people would have been, and like it or not, I won't let you wreck that good impression."

Before he could do more than mutter angrily she'd turned and stepped out to the street.

"Dawn?"

She stopped short, turned. Wes had followed her out into Central Avenue. He stood there tensely, his mouth a grim line, his red-brown eyes looking oddly tormented.

"Yes, Wes?" she asked.

"I think," he said, "that you had better have dinner with me. I won't kiss you or otherwise embarrass you, you know that. But I do have rights. Rights as a human being, if nothing else, or even rights as an old friend. What about dinner in George and Molly's on the pier?"

Dawn caught her breath. Were she to say no he'd give a shrug and that would be that. She'd not see him again.

"Well?" Wes asked.

Dawn nodded.

Wes turned and locked the door of his small brick office building. He then stepped across the sidewalk and lightly took her arm. "A nice evening," he said, "wouldn't you call it? I'll be sorry when daylight saving time comes along."

41

"Why?"

"It seems unnatural. Why don't we walk to the pier? It'll give us a good appetite."

Dawn was scandalized. "Wes, I'll be darned if I'll date you in work clothes. You'll pick me up at the house in an hour, so there."

She refused to be talked out of it, either. A fellow, she thought, was at least entitled to the illusion of romance.

Fatefully, Dawn got into her car and drove back to her home to dress.

Chapter VI

SHE HAD FOUR DINNERS WITH WES IN THE TWO WEEKS THAT followed, and several people approved. One such person was the elderly lady who lived next door. Mrs. Elliott wasn't averse to saying so, either. Nor was she averse to invading the March patio to say so. One Saturday morning Dawn heard the gate in the side fence creak open and click shut. When she looked over her shoulder she saw Mrs. Elliott standing near the orange tree and glancing around with interest. She gave the woman a broad smile. "Hi," she said. "Want coffee?"

"It's a lovely patio, girl. I don't approve of the attempt to create a formal Japanese garden, however. What's wrong with just a good old-fashioned California patio?"

"Nothing."

"Well, then?"

"It's exercise for Mom, though. She'll be tubby if she doesn't exercise. Obesity is unhealthful. So Pop says she may have a formal Japanese garden. Subtle?"

Mrs. Elliott walked over to one of the wicker lawn chairs before the ornamental pool. She sat down, crossed her legs comfortably. "I notice that you're the one who's creating the pool, however. Why don't you ask Wes to help you?"

Dawn chuckled, a young and engaging sight in her Bermuda shorts and yellow blouse. "He claims he's busy trying to sell the Klingley farm to a man named Bush."

"I understand you've had several dates with him recently."

"Well, we have had several dinners together."

"An entirely worthy young man. You have to admit, girl, that when Wes makes up his mind to love someone he's a difficult fellow to distract."

"Well . . ."

"No shameful, hard-living, self-centered woman for him! No Mrs. Clara Royce—not for him! A dreadful woman. I met her at the club several days ago. She's going to settle down in Port West, it seems, and there she was cooing at all of us and trying to ingratiate her way into our good graces."

Dawn straightened up, and dug her fingers into the cramped muscles just above her hips. She worked her thumbs around vigorously to relieve the muscle tension. She'd worked in that half-crouch too long! And she'd worked too darned hard, also! Now her mother would have to take over, do her share. It wasn't the daughter, after all, who needed to lose weight.

Mrs. Elliott wasn't easily ignored. "I told Mrs. Royce," Mrs. Elliott announced, "that Port West is a friendly town that is always happy to welcome decent, friendly people into the fold. And I also told this Mrs. Royce that we of Port West reserve judgment."

"I think you ought to feel ashamed."

"Why?"

"Because you were rude."

"I doubt," Mrs. Elliott said dryly, "that Mrs. Royce even noticed it. Dr. Ken Jones was coming along at the time, and Mrs. Royce seemed to be more interested in that fact."

Dawn took a chair in the patch of shade cast by the orange tree. She considered the scrap of information Mrs. Elliott had given her. Oddly, she was depressed by the fact that Ken was still seeing the experienced beauty. Why was that, eh? What in the world had she expected? Surely she wasn't so naïve as to think Ken would change his mind about Mrs. Royce just like that? She shook her tousled brunette head, loosed a sigh.

"Anyway," she said, "you're old enough to know that only boors are rude. Did you want something?"

The frail Mrs. Elliott gave a chuckle. "Now that you ask, girl, I wonder if you have some extra eggs. I'm expecting my granddaughter this afternoon. She has developed the most ridiculous passion for eggs."

"Mom always has extras. Want a dozen? I'll be going into town this afternoon. It seems that Dan Colby always runs short of eggs, too."

"Dan Colby?"

"The fellow who has the salvage concession at the dump."

The gray eyes gleamed, out there in the sun. The frail figure, which had half risen from the wicker chair, froze into temporary rigidity. Then it dropped down. "I hadn't heard

44

there was such a thing as a salvage concession at the dump, girl. And what's your connection with Dan Colby?"

"A patient. He wrenched his knee quite severely, and there were other complications. He's quite an artist, incidentally, if you ever want to buy a painting."

"Now that seems a strange way for an artist to earn his living. Is he one of those modern artists who paint pictures of rubbish and such?"

Dawn had to smile. "I think that Dan Colby would shoot you dead for even suggesting that. Actually, he concentrates on the ocean and the creatures of the ocean and beach. Wes has a few of his paintings, and they're good."

"I didn't know Wes appreciated art."

But at that moment they were interrupted. Dawn's mother came out the back door, presumably to work. For the occasion she wore a new pair of levi slacks and a short-sleeved cotton blouse. A new cap adorned her head, a new pair of white cotton gloves adorned her hands. Looking down critically at the ornamental pool her daughter had begun to fashion, she shook her head. "But the design is too rigid, dear. The Japanese are never that rigid in their art. It should have a free, flowing form, and no pun intended."

Dawn went into the house and got a box of eggs from the cooler. A glance at the kitchen clock told her it was later than she'd thought, and she supposed she ought to clean up and change her clothes before she made the drive into Oxton to pick up her father at his office. Upstairs in her room, however, she found their Saturday woman of all work giving the place one of her more thorough cleanings. "Miss Dawn," Mrs. Regan asked, "why are you letting your poor mother do all that work? A big strong girl like you? If you ask me, I think it's a real shame."

The room, at this stage of the cleaning process, looked as if a cyclone had struck it. The two armchairs and the dresser had been shoved over to one of the windows. The vanity-table had been picked up bodily by the mighty Mrs. Regan and laid across the bed. Half the carpet had been rolled back to give Mrs. Regan plenty of working room, and Mrs. Regan was apparently intent upon eradicating the last suggestion of dirt from the walls, the ceiling, the floor. She dipped her cleaning sponge into her pail, swung about and proceeded to work on the wall. "What I always say," she said, "is this,

45

A girl don't keep her Ma forever, so a girl had oughta be nice to her Ma while she can."

"This doesn't have to be hospital clean, you know."

Mrs. Regan loosed a deep belly laugh. "It's my system, Miss Dawn. I give it a cleaning like this three times a year; then the rest of the year it ain't much work to speak of."

"Just the same—"

"Was you wanting something up here?"

Dawn changed her mind about getting into more suitable clothes. Nor did she have the nerve to clean up in the bathroom between the two bedrooms. She'd be certain to leave a grayish smear of dirt somewhere; then there'd be an explosion!

"No," she fibbed, "I just wanted to see how you were getting along."

She retreated to the patio. She gave Mrs. Elliott the box of eggs and continued to the garage at the rear of the lot. She invaded her father's hobby shed behind the garage and did her cleaning up at his wash sink. Only fifteen minutes behind schedule, she backed her car to the street and headed inland to Oxton. It was in her father's reception room that she met the second person who approved of the dates she was having with Wes Overton. Harriette Jones looked up, gave a grin, closed the *Life* magazine she'd been reading. "Hi, Dawn. I was hoping I'd see you."

"What in the world are you doing in here?"

"Waiting for you. Couldn't your father do his own driving?"

Dawn gave it some thought. "Well, he won't like it, but he won't shoot me. Wait here and I'll see."

She opened the door across the reception room and took the short hall to the big office at the end. She caught her father whittling. He was abashed. He then recovered his aplomb and actually held the wood up to give her a good look at it. "A giraffe," he told her. "A very pleasant way to relax, incidentally. I strongly favor hobbies such as this. All of us possess an instinctive yearning to create, and—"

"You told Ma you had a very busy morning ahead of you."

He met her steady brown eyes. He smiled faintly. "Well, apparently most of my patients recovered during the night. How is the pool coming along?"

"Pop, aren't you ashamed?"

He closed his big whittling knife and laid it away in the middle drawer of his desk. He pushed his desk chair back

46

and nonchalantly crossed his legs. "Well," he said carefully, "you know how your mother is. She's a dear woman, and I treasure her greatly, but she does have a helpless quality, and I'm always foolish enough to want to help her. But suppose I did help her? Would she be slimmed down, toned up by the exercise, or would I?"

Dawn had to concede his point was well taken. Furthermore, she thought, he did enough for his family and for his community right there where he was. That was the other side of the coin that Wes never saw. If her father did like to have his own way, he also liked to provide his family with the luxuries and comforts that would keep them hale, hearty and happy. "Ah, relax," she told him. "I won't tattle. Hattie Jones is outside and she wants me to have lunch with her. Would you mind driving home alone?"

"Certainly not."

Dawn blinked. Her face took on the expression of a startled child. She dropped into an armchair and stared. "Will you say that again?"

"My dear child," said Dr. Roger March, "I am certainly not an unreasonable man. This is your day off. You have every right to spend that day off however you choose to spend it."

Up front, the bell over the entrance door tinkled. Dawn waited, then remembered that Miss Graves didn't work Saturday mornings any more. She jumped up and went down the hall to the reception room. It was old Mr. Dodd, a bony little man in his customary pair of baggy black pants. His shoe-button eyes twinkled. "Howdy, Dawn. You coming fishing with your Pa an' me?"

"Fishing?"

Mr. Dodd nodded zestfully. "Got us a good spot, Dawn, over t' the old Oxton pier. Lots of buttermouth perch waitin' t' be caught, you ask me."

"I see."

She turned to go back to give her father a piece of her mind, but the second trip up the hall wasn't necessary. Her father came into the pleasantly furnished reception room, and he was looking abashed again. He could think quickly, however, and did. "Now listen," he said, after he'd appraised the situation. "I would have told you what I did about your day off even if I'd not made arrangements to go fishing with

Dodd. Confound it, I'm beginning to resent these insinuations that I'm a—well, a tyrant. Preposterous! Utterly preposterous!"

Dawn didn't argue the matter. She gave Harriette Jones a little nod, and Harriette got up and led the way out to the street. A few minutes later, in Harriette's car, they were driving at a snail's pace along one of the rural roads toward the dry, rolling hill country beyond Oxton. Harriette came to the point very quickly.

"You're using your intelligence, Dawn. Ken seems to have heard about your dates with Wes. And he's disturbed. He thinks I don't know, of course."

"Oh?"

The road thinned somewhat to cut through a great orange grove. For acre after acre on either side of the road the grove stretched, and it was a magnificent sight in the late April sunshine.

Harriette said gravely, "Of course you wouldn't want to encourage Wes to the point of hurting him, but it would be a clever idea if you were to continue to date him. My brother is a peculiar person in one respect. He has tremendous pride. I think that if he were given the idea that you could get along very nicely without him . . ."

"You think that's why I'm seeing Wes?"

Harriette's large gray eyes seemed to become even larger. Her forehead puckered into a network of questioning lines. "But isn't that why you're seeing him?"

Dawn swallowed, it suddenly occurring to her that probably others thought the same thing. But great day in the morning, they were wrong! She might be seeing more of Wes because now she had more time, but certainly their relations hadn't changed. She'd given Wes no reason to think that they would change, either. They'd just been old friends eating together, talking together, riding together. Good heavens, she might be many rotten things, but she certainly wasn't the type of girl who'd take advantage of anyone for reasons of strategy!

Harriette seemed to understand that, too. She gave a quick, warm smile. "Sorry. And that brings me to the reason I sat waiting for you in your father's office. I think you ought to preen your feathers and come to the house for dinner next week."

Pink rushed to Dawn's cheeks. "Oh, I don't know—"

"You do love my brother, don't you?"

48

"Of course I do. But—"

Very firmly, Harriette shook her head. "Then you have no choice. I think that dating Wes has helped you, but I also think that seeing Ken again will help you, too. Anyway, what do you have to lose?"

Love was a queer thing, Dawn thought. Why had she fallen in love?

Chapter VII

SHE WAS EXCITED, DAN NOTICED, AND QUITE OBVIOUSLY
not herself. He disapproved. An excited, abstracted person
obviously wasn't in harmony with the world.

"Any problems, Miss March?" he asked. "I've dealt with
problems before. Perhaps I can help you with this one."

She turned, gave a half-smile. Dan liked that half-smile, and
it suddenly occurred to him that actually he liked Miss Dawn
March. He liked the clean, wholesome lines of her figure, her
asymetrical face with its dignity, deep brown eyes, pleasantly
formed mouth. In her way, he reflected, she was quite a
beauty. And it was a beauty that counted because it was as
much an inner thing, a thing of the mind, the spirit, as it
was a thing compounded of pink and cream skin and all
that. He was puzzled. A girl so lovely, so obviously decent
and well-intentioned, ought to have been married long before
this. What had happened? Was that her problem?

"I missed you yesterday," he told her. "It's peculiar, isn't
it, how quickly one becomes accustomed to changes? I seem
to have become accustomed to seeing you every other morning around ten."

"I had some work to do at the office. One of the banes of
our existence is the paper work we have to do toward the
end of each month."

He nodded, understanding the tone of her voice because
he had quite often reacted to paper work in precisely that way.
In fact, he mused, it had been that reaction to paper work
among other things that had finally precipitated the revolu-
tion. One morning, in his office in New York City, he had
looked at the thick sheaf of papers on his desk and decided
that he'd starve before he'd so much as look at a spec or a
report or a recommendation or a memo.

"Care to see a painting?" he asked.

"Of what?"

"Merely a wave. It isn't a wave to rival the wave done by Monet, but it isn't a static gob of green paint, either."

She went to a chair in her nicely poised way and sat down and smoothed her gray skirt over her knees. Now she looked like a child about to be given a rare treat. "I've been hoping you'd offer to show me some of your paintings, Dan. A fellow I know, Wes Overton, has several of your things hanging in his office."

Dan was interested to perceive that she suddenly looked less abstracted and considerably happier. Now there was a sparkle in her deep brown eyes, liveliness in the very way she sat on her chair. He did some probing.

"Know Wes very well, Miss March?"

"We more or less grew up together. He's only a year older than I, and for some reason we always hit it off well as children."

Then this was the woman Wes had often talked about, but never named? Enormously interested now, Dan lit a cigarette and did some quick thinking. As he remembered the story, the woman Wes loved was infatuated with some other man. "Screwy," Wes had termed the infatuation, "because she doesn't know that guy one half as well as she thinks she does. But don't worry; she'll see him for the guy he is and then it'll be my turn, pal."

Perhaps the thing Wes had predicted had come to pass.

"A nice fellow, Wes," Dan said thoughtfully. "You might describe Wes as being in complete harmony with the world. You seldom meet a person who is. Wes was very kind to me, Miss March. That will explain why he has so many of my paintings. I don't usually part with my paintings."

"Why not?"

"Perhaps because the subjects mean a great deal to me. Or perhaps because expression of any kind is too personal a thing to sell. I don't know."

"Other artists have been able to sell their paintings. Perhaps they discovered something you should discover, that all life is a kind of compromise."

Dan said flatly: "I think people are wrong to compromise."

"Why?"

She had the same sort of mind, he decided, that his father had. Bend to the storm! Sell your heart's blood, if necessary, to provide material comforts for the rest of your body! And

51

live, therefore, without dignity, without meaning! Disappointed in her, he gave a shrug. "It's a long story," he told her, "and I'm sure you have other patients to see."

There was a silence of perhaps five minutes. She simply sat quietly on her chair, studying him as he probably studied a sea bird. He disliked being studied that way, but he endured it good-humoredly. Had he ever been concerned about what others thought, he reflected, he would still be his father's executive vice president in New York City. To each human being his own way of life, to each human being the opportunity to work out his destiny as best he could—what did it matter what others thought or said?

The silence was ended by the powerful rumble of an engine. Miss Dawn March stood up, glanced at her wristwatch, then went with her attractive grace to her kit on the table. She lifted the heavy leather kit almost effortlessly, and with practised hands got it nicely hung from her shoulder. Then she startled him.

"I'll see you next week, Dan. There's very little I can do for you. It's merely a question of checking up from time to time."

"Oh?"

"Of course, should you ever need me, you have only to let me know. Our slogan is service with a smile when you need service."

Then she was gone. In a twinkling, Dan Colby felt oddly alone and restless. Sitting on the studio couch, he looked down glumly at his injured leg. It was doing all right he supposed. Certainly much of the swelling had been reduced and much of the soreness had been eased from the bones and muscles. Still, it was all taking too long. Already he'd missed April, and how could he be certain he'd not miss much of May? A fellow couldn't paint indoors. The light was wretched. Moreover, a remembered wave or bird or fish or sea lion or sand dune was never as useful to an artist as the thing itself. A remembered wave wasn't a true wave. It was but an impression, at best, merely a remembered quality. An artist needed something more substantial to work with. What it came down to, in short, was that if an artist wanted to paint the world he had to be outdoors looking at the world as it was, not as an impression it was making.

He looked up, hearing a familiar step outside. So that was why Miss March had gone out so quickly? Dan grinned. As Wes strode in, Dan gave a solemn wag of his black head. "You ought to be ashamed of yourself, fellow. Obvious tactics won't ever win the fair lady."

Big Wes gave a booming chuckle and set a crate of groceries on the floor. "A guy has to do what he can, chum. I think I remembered everything. Say, what about getting outdoors into the sun?"

Dan got up with alacrity, balancing himself on one leg. Wes got the crutch, and with the help of the big real estate broker and the crutch Dan managed to hobble outdoors to a chair. He looked hungrily across the beach at the ocean. This May morning the ocean was a royal blue and almost as placid as a mill pond. Off to the right, in the clear air, he could see Anacapa and Santa Cruz Islands lifting their bulks toward the sky. The islands, too, were a royal blue because of some illusion created by the light being reflected from the water. Some day, he thought, he would have to paint those islands.

"Want some news?" Wes asked.

"Not particularly."

Wes ran a big hand through his curly brown hair. He laughed softly, wonderingly. "You really don't care what goes on in the world around you, do you?"

"It's a question of interest, isn't it? I doubt you know nearly as much about this segment of the world spread before you as I do about Port West and vicinity. The Caspian terns are back, for example. Do you know what a Caspian tern is?"

"I was talking about human beings, chum."

Dan grinned. "I know that Miss March is feeling disturbed, fellow. I also know that she's very fond of you. Have a spat?"

"Huh?"

Dan dismissed that possibility. The big lug wore his emotions on his face. He could no more dissemble successfully than a clam could fly.

"An interesting girl," he said to the big fellow. "Did you know that she's a crackerjack nurse?"

"She ought to be. The trouble with the March family is that they have but one interest, and that involves the sick, the maimed, the dying. When they first came here, Dawn's mother

53

worked as a nurse in Oxton Hospital. Dawn was trained to be a nurse almost from the day she took her first step."

"You sound bitter."

The reddish-brown eyes flared. "Sure I am. We'd be married by now if she'd not gone to Los Angeles and entered training school. We were all set, chum. But when she came back, things were different. She was a girl with a mission, suddenly, and the first thing I knew she was having a career as a nurse."

"Someone has to do the dirty work."

"And someone has to marry, have kids, or there won't be a world to work in. Look, I have this whole thing figured out. This work she does—it mixes her up. She forgets that what's important is living life in the round. Look, I know exactly what she's going through. When I'm involved in a deal I tend to think of nothing but that deal. I almost live that deal, in fact. And that's what she does. Only her work goes on and on, and I don't have deals twenty-four hours of the day. You catch?"

A pelican came winging across the sky. He was a raggle-taggle creature that looked all beak and ruffled feathers and legs. Then the pelican peeled off and dove and was suddenly a very efficient instrument of destruction. It hit the water with a splash, and when it lifted its head from the water a fish was wriggling in its beak. Dan wondered how many pelicans he'd seen diving for their food. He wondered how many he'd tried to paint, and always in vain.

"Well, never mind," Wes said cheerfully. "It moves. It isn't as I want it yet, but it moves. Listen, I know of a person who'd like to buy a seagull. I asked five hundred, and this person didn't bat an eyelash. Care to earn five hundred bucks?"

"No."

That annoyed the big fellow, as always. The cheerful smile faded from his lips. He took a deep breath, then swung around forcefully to argue the matter. The argument, when it was delivered, was the usual one. Money was important. And it was wise to sell a few things, because when you did so others saw your work and gradually you picked up a reputation. The reputation brought you good commissions. Eventually, you had all the money you needed to live comfortably, even as an artist. You didn't have to live in a dump, literally,

54

and you didn't have to take time from your work to run that dump, either.

Dan nodded at appropriate times, but hardly listened. He was too engrossed in the emotional problem of this big fellow who'd given him a lift when he'd needed it. Surely there was something a disinterested person such as he could do to give the big fellow a helping hand. Obviously, Dawn March wasn't quite as happy with her career as Wes Overton apparently thought. Therefore—

"For five hundred bucks," Wes finally concluded his argument, "you ought to climb down from your artistic high horse."

"Why the seagull?" Dan asked.

"How should I know? This fellow stopped into my office to talk about buying some land. He saw the painting. He took the painting from the wall and carried it out to the street. He must have stood there studying the thing for almost a half-hour."

Dan's black brows came together. "That long?"

"He knew art, all right. He said something to the effect that you had an extraordinarily effective technique. And he went on and on about your beautiful sense of composition. Did you know you have a beautiful sense of composition?"

Dan was intrigued. "What else did he have to say?"

"Well, he wanted your address, among other things. I didn't give him that, because at the back of my crassly commercial mind was the thought he'd lower the offered bid the moment he saw this place."

"Not the money," Dan growled irritably. "What did he say about the painting?"

"Well, he did seem to think that you'd overdone the feathers."

That surprised Dan. He tucked it away in the back of his mind to think about later on. "Any other criticisms?"

The reddish-brown eyes began to twinkle. "Okay," Wes said good-naturedly, "if your ego needs a boost he thinks you have a great talent. Those were his exact words. So he wants to see you, see some more of your work. And he'd like to buy a seagull for five hundred dollars."

"Well, I'll think about it. Now you'd better get me back indoors. The groceries ought to be put away."

They put in a busy ten minutes, and Wes had a can of beer and did some more talking about his girl and finally left. Dan listened, and when he was certain the car had left the dump he eased himself down to the floor and slid across the floor to the large closet off the kitchenette. He found the paintings he wanted and stood them up against a wall, then slid backward a dozen or so feet to study them. For a time he was puzzled by the criticism the prospective customer had made of his treatment of feathers. The feathers were true in just about every particular he could think of. And then it occurred to him that perhaps the very trueness of the feathers had inspired the criticism. Perhaps his treatment of them had been too photographic.

A fellow would have to watch that, Dan decided.

It was quite possible that his passion for detail was running away with him.

Chapter VIII

The HOUSE IN MARICOPA STREET WAS RUDDY IN THE
sunset when Dawn again got out of her car to have dinner with
Ken and his sister. There was no wind to speak of, and the
usual rumble of the surf had been noticeably reduced to faint
crashings. Up the street several boys were playing catch.
They were obviously intent upon playing softball, because
each was practicing an underhand delivery. She was startled
to think that the softball season would soon come again to California. What had happened to the winter? Where had all the
winter months gone? Why, pretty soon now it would be time
to think about vacations!

She opened the gate and stepped into the Jones yard. Much
gardening had been done since her last visit, she saw, and all
of it had been quite effective.

She pressed the bell-button, heard the chimes, heard Ken's
footsteps coming to the door. Her heart thumped. She felt herself go hot, felt her nerves tingle, and was considerably vexed.
This was ridiculous! This was adolescent stuff, and she was
standing on the brink of twenty-five. Disgraceful!

Yet when the door opened, she was glad she could and did
react to Ken in precisely that adolescent way. This, she saw
quickly, was the Ken she'd come to love, a good-looking man
with a warm smile, warm gray eyes and a nice air of merriness
and dash. He fell back a step and took her measure. Did he
approve of her in yellow and brown? He did!

"You know," he said in his musical baritone, "you grow
lovelier with each passing hour. Nice to see you again, Dawn."

"Nice to see you again, Ken."

He stepped back from the door, ushered her inside the
square foyer. The door on her left was standing partially ajar,
and she glimpsed someone in the dental chair. She compressed
her lips, wondering how long Ken would be kept busy.

He noticed her expression, pulled the office door shut. "An
extraction," he said casually. "The old story of postponing a

visit to a dentist until it's too late. Now he'll lose a tooth I might have saved."

He gestured her into the living-room ahead of him. This was an occasion, it developed, because several vases of flowers were in evidence, and the best Jones crystal wine glasses were standing on the best Jones sterling silver serving tray.

"Hattie?" Ken called. "Want a sherry?"

Harriette came in quickly, an apron tied about her middle, her face flushed, her blonde hair slightly disarrayed. "Hi," she grinned. "Ken, we'd better wait until you've handled that extraction. Anyway, dinner will be a bit late, too. Dawn, guess where I spent half the afternoon?"

Ken gave a mock sigh but turned and left them to their "female" chatter.

"Just at the local clink, that's all," Harriette said. She paused dramatically to let that sink in, then hurried on. "I got to thinking about Mr. Dover. I got to remembering how very nice he was to Ken and me when we first came to Port West. And I thought that maybe at a time like this it would do him good to see a friendly face, so I just upped and drove over to our local clink."

Dawn sat down on the couch and nodded. "Good for you."

Harriette grimaced. "It wasn't such a pleasant experience, though. A jail's a very grim place. I mean, there are the bars, and you can't help but think of animals in cages. And there Mr. Dover was just sitting and staring at the three blank walls. They can't even see out the windows, Dawn, because the window in each cell is almost up at the ceiling."

"Did he have anything to say?"

"Not much. He's different, Dawn. He seems all squeezed in physically and mentally, if you know what I mean. I don't think he really cares what happens to him."

A letting go? But why, if he were innocent? Or perhaps the truth was that he wasn't innocent.

"He asked about his wife," Harriette said. "I told him she was bearing up well, but she isn't, poor thing. And then he asked what people were saying—that sort of thing."

No, Dawn decided, Mr. Dover wasn't letting go. A person who was concerned about the things others were saying . . . well, that person must assuredly still have some hope and fight and determination left in him. Her pulse quickened. She felt very pleased with Mr. Dover, suddenly.

"What about a lawyer?" she asked. "Has he hired one?"

"No money."

"Doesn't the county appoint a lawyer in such an event?"

"I suppose so. But what kind of lawyer? You know how such things are bound to work. Usually the lawyers who hang around waiting for such assignments are beginners who have to get practice and money somehow. Do you know what I think?"

"What?"

"He'll need a very good lawyer, Dawn, a much better lawyer than the court will appoint."

Dawn swallowed hard. Harriette wasn't just talking idly. Harriette wasn't that sort. So that meant there was a darned strong possibility Mr. Dover would spend years in a jail. And that meant, in turn, that poor Mrs. Dover . . .

She jumped up, and on an impulse hurried to the telephone. She dialed Sammy Berman's number in Oxton and kept his telephone ringing until he finally answered it in self-defense. When he learned it was Dawn March calling he loosed a mock groan. "Sure," he said, "one of your lame ducks is in trouble again, I'll bet you a dime."

"Sammy, is that nice?"

His tenor voice almost rose a full octave. "Nice, she asks! Do you telephone, do you come to see the wife and kids when you don't have a lame duck in trouble?"

"I've been busy. You'd be surprised to know how busy I've been."

He wasn't to be charmed into quick forgiveness, nor was he to be easily distracted from his point. "I will bet you a nickel," he said sternly, "that you now have a lame duck in trouble."

Dawn flushed.

"Well?" he demanded.

She shrugged, wet her lips, made the plunge. "Mr. Dover could use a lawyer, Sammy. You've heard of the case, no doubt?"

Tomfoolery stopped. "Forget it," he snapped. "I had lunch with the D. A. himself the other afternoon, and the D. A. is purring with satisfaction. Which means, in the event you don't know, that he has the Dover case sewed up tight."

"I didn't know that."

"Well, that's how it is. Sure, I could step in, but the best I could do for Dover would be to suggest that he plead guilty. It's his first offense, he's had his problems, and the judge would probably be sympathetic. A couple of years, a parole . . . well, that's the best he could hope for."

Ken came back into the living-room. "The deed is done," he said, and then he noticed that Dawn was using the telephone. He went over to the couch, a good-looking figure of a man in a light gray gabardine suit. He imperiously gestured Harriette back toward her kitchen, and after Harriette had left, Ken opened the bottle of sherry and filled the three crystal glasses.

Sammy Berman's voice recalled Dawn's mind to the more serious business at hand. "Oh, I'll do it," he said, "if Dover wants me as his lawyer. Talk it over with him, and let me know."

"Thanks, Sammy. How's Ruth?"

"I'm glad to hear," he said sarcastically, "that you remember Ruth exists. Why don't you drop in to see her some year soon?"

Dawn laughed dutifully and told him she might surprise him and cradled the telephone. She went back to the couch, aware of Ken's admiring eyes, aware that this evening wouldn't be the flop one other evening had been. "That was Sammy Berman. Remember him? He's the lawyer who helps us with our legal problems."

"Quite a fellow, I understand. Who's the person in trouble this time?"

"Mr. Dover. Harriette saw him in jail this afternoon."

"Oh, I see." Ken handed her a glass, and picked up one for himself. "To beauty," he toasted, as of old, "and it's very nice to have you here, too."

Dawn settled back and sipped the sherry. She had but one regret now that his gaze was upon her and that smile was back on his lips. The regret was that she'd not arranged for this meeting sooner.

Ken pursed his lips and seemed to search his mind for exactly the appropriate words. Then he said quite simply, "I like to see you, Dawn. I'll always like to see you, in fact."

She looked down at her lap. She saw, or thought she saw, a speck of dust on her brown, yellow-piped skirt. With her

60

neatly manicured forefinger nail she flicked, or thought she did, that speck of dust from the material.

Ken spoke on quietly, intent upon her face. "Then why did I behave as I did, say the things I did? Well, it's possible that even a dentist can occasionally feel the strain of a tricky piece of dental surgery. I don't offer that as an excuse, really. It's merely an explanation."

Dawn looked up, but didn't speak.

Ken smiled. "Oh, I don't deny that Mrs. Clara Royce is an attractive woman. She is. Moreover, she's a fascinating woman because she has done many things and has seen many places. And she has a good business head on her shoulders. Did you suspect that when you met her?"

"I think I noticed her beauty, and that she had a clear concept of what she wanted. I didn't notice anything else."

"You never do notice the more disagreeable traits a person has, do you? Anyway, I have been seeing a great deal of her, but I think I ought to explain at this point that I have been doing so for business reasons. You see, Dawn, I haven't the slightest intention of being a Port West dentist for the rest of my life."

She took another sip of the wine. It was good wine, she knew, but she didn't like it. Nor did she like talking about Mrs. Clara Royce. This was an evening for fun! This was an evening for a good dinner, then dancing, then all the rest. He'd made his explanation, she'd not argued the matter, so why didn't he forget the rest?

Ken set his glass down and rose and paced restlessly over to the fireplace. "A dentist can be big or small," he told her, "just like any other person. He can work in a small town like this for a bare living, or he can operate in many small towns like this for big money. I've always felt that I could have a chain of dental offices throughout southern California if I could just obtain a little backing."

"You're not serious!"

He whirled, his gray eyes narrowed. "Quite serious. Business is good all over. Others have found chains to be practical and profitable. Would you care to look at some figures?"

Dawn quickly shook her head. "Absolutely not. I think you should work as my father works, for something other than purely personal gain. And that's how you used to think, Ken."

61

Almost in dreaming tones he said: "Mrs. Royce has the capital, Dawn. She was married three times, in the event you didn't know, and each time she was awarded a big divorce settlement. Now she has capital she'd like to invest."

"I see."

"But you really don't see, isn't that true?"

Dawn stood up, thinking she'd like to go into the kitchen at that point to do some talking with Harriette. But Ken was still talking and she had to listen, of course.

"As I was saying," he went on, "you can't really see because it isn't that apparent. When I said she has capital she'd like to invest I was telling the truth. Surely you don't think for an instant that she'd have to come to a town such as this to buy a husband such as I?"

It was a difficult question for Dawn to answer. She didn't know Mrs. Royce well enough even to hazard a guess as to what the woman had in her mind. Yet she instinctively knew that much of this big talk hadn't been hatched in the mind of Ken Jones. She did think she knew him well enough to be sure of that. Just a month ago, for instance, he'd been happily talking about the pleasure he found in living and working in Port West. Then, quite suddenly, here he was talking in grandiose terms and dreaming grandiose dreams.

"Ken, how did you meet her?"

"Quite simple." He laughed, as if relieved that the subject had been changed. "She needed some tricky work done, and a former patient, now living in Los Angeles, recommended me. She drove here, I did the work, and she's still here."

"I understand she's planning to stay here."

"She will if I can talk her into it. Listen, Dawn, I'm quite serious about trying to establish a chain of offices in at least this section of California. The woods are full of dentists who need experience before they open offices of their own. They can be hired on a fifty-fifty basis, or something like that. For my fifty per cent I'd supply the offices, the equipment, the advertising."

"Buy your new teeth now, pay later—that sort of thing?"

"Well, why not?"

"Because it isn't the sort of life for you, for one thing. And because it wouldn't be fair to the patients, either. But you know all that."

He smiled, his gray eyes thoughtful. "Perhaps the difficulty is that I don't know all that. At any rate, I'd not take anything Mrs. Royce said that evening too seriously. Clara has a dreadful failing, if you must know. It involves her ego. I think she automatically resents it whenever a person she knows shows any interest in someone else."

"I see."

Harriette came out to claim her glass of sherry. She saw them standing together near the fireplace and gave a nod to signify her approval. "After dinner," she said generously, "you may go out to dance. I'll take a walk along the beach. Oh, and that reminds me, Dawn. I understand you're functioning as a nurse to Dan Colby. Would he welcome a visitor, do you think?"

"I wouldn't know. Why not just barge in?"

Ken wanted to know who Dan Colby was, and it was his sister who told him. Ken was interested. How could any man who had a shred of self-respect be content to live like a bum on the raggle-taggle edge of the ocean? He announced that Dan Colby ought to have his head examined. And back he went to his grandiose talk and grandiose dream, and it was that way the rest of the evening. Around midnight, when Dawn finally got back home, she was heartily sick of anything involving ambition. To her mother's questioning eyes in the living-room she said: "No, I didn't enjoy myself at all." And wondering why that was, and wishing it hadn't been like that, she moodily went upstairs to bed. She couldn't help wondering, as she undressed, why Ken had spent so long an evening telling her such outright fibs. Disinterested in Clara Royce? Now that was ridiculous. Perhaps he didn't love Clara Royce, but he certainly wasn't indifferent to her, either.

Chapter IX

It WAS DAN COLBY, ODDLY ENOUGH, WHO ANSWERED THE question for her. It happened almost a week later. Feeling a need for exercise and a chance to think, Dawn was walking along the beach and admiring the waves when someone gave her a hail. She looked left, and there was her artist patient grinning down at her from a sand dune. She hustled over to the sand dune and glared back at Dan Colby. "Aren't you pleased?" she demanded. "You'll probably be crippled permanently."

"As my father would say, arrant nonsense."

"You were given strict orders not to use that knee until you were given an okay."

"I prefer you in shorts," Dan Colby countered. "In spirit, I bow to your beauty."

Dawn was flabbergasted speechless.

Dan gestured. "It's fine up here, Miss March. From this coign of vantage one may see many worthwhile sights. A few minutes ago I actually saw a whale disporting himself over yonder."

Dawn had to get up onto the sand dune to take a look. She'd never seen a whale of any kind doing anything, and she was suddenly as excited as any kid.

"That's more like it," Dan Colby told her. "But to set the record straight, Wes Overton huffed and puffed me up to this coign of vantage and he'll be coming back for me around ten. I have been learning things. Some day I shall paint the things I have learned. You looked happy, incidentally."

Dawn sat down beside him. She felt the pull of Dan's personality but she was careful not to allow him to perceive that. She said coolly, methodically, "Nevertheless, Dan, you ought to check with me before you undertake expeditions of any kind. Your knee has come along nicely. Another few weeks—well, you can afford to be patient. You have no responsibility to carry, have you?"

He gave a laugh, but he was obviously annoyed with her. He picked a handful of sand from the dune and tossed it on the beach. "Nicely put, Miss March. You should know my father. My father was also an adept in the art of delivering a nasty crack."

Dawn, her face stony, kept silent.

A fairly large wave came rolling in to break thunderously on the beach. Spindrift rose, sparkled briefly in the sunlight, faded from sight. Perhaps a hundred yards beyond the breakers, the snout of a sea lion came pushing from the water, then the entire head of the creature. The wet head sparkled in the sunlight as the spindrift had.

"To each his own," Dan Colby said tensely. "I could make out a good case against your way of life. I don't. Why not? Because it seems to me it would be impertinent of me to say how you should live."

"I carry my weight, Dan. Do you?"

He laughed shortly. "A good point. Well, do I or don't I? You give a person something beautiful to see, to enjoy. Is that carrying your weight, or isn't it?"

"Why did your father make the nasty cracks, Dan?"

"Probably because he felt disappointed in me." Dan raised a hand, scratched his head. His black hair was very long now, and Dawn wondered how she could contrive to get him a haircut. Probably the easiest way to accomplish it would be to send Nicky to him. But that would be expensive.

"Why did he feel disappointed in you, Dan? Incidentally, I don't intend to be a snoop. But I have worked over you for a time, now, and I'm afraid patients always become human beings to me in the end. I hate to think that when all this is over you'll settle back into your rut."

"Let's simply say," Dan said, "that I didn't share his interest in business. Ironically enough, my sister does share that interest, but of course my father is totally unaware of that— and would be shocked if he knew. An old-fashioned man in many respects. Home and babies for the girl children, business and papa's footsteps for the boy children."

"I see."

"You can't apply the term rut to my life, either, Miss March. It seems to me that I have a pleasant existence, one with considerable point. I paint. I work very hard to learn what I need to know. I grow. Now precisely what is wrong with all that?"

"And how do you live?"

"Perhaps society is to blame. Perhaps in another society there would be room for people who like to paint."

"Or isn't that the easy way out? Blame society, and therefore excuse yourself from blame. You're wrong, however, because surely there are markets for artists."

"Paint what they ask you to paint?"

Dawn's lips twitched. She didn't quite laugh, however. Experience told her that laughing at him now would undo much of the work she'd done to pull his personality out of its shell. "The trouble with that kind of reasoning may be this, Dan: that you're now in effect saying that if you cannot have life on your own terms you won't participate in life."

"One paints what he has to paint, Dawn March. Or works as a nurse if one has to be a nurse."

"Others, you see, effect a compromise with life. This much they do for their daily bread; this much they do to fulfill their obligation to society; and this much they do for their personal development and pleasure. Catch?"

"My," he said, "we are wise, aren't we?"

The sea lion disappeared, as if tired of being ignored. For a minute or two there was little to see except sand and water and sky. Then a flock of sanderlings came flying along and alighted on the beach to feed. They skittered toward the ocean and back from the ocean as the surf pushed inland, then receded. They kept themselves very busy. Now they poked their bills down into the wet sand, now they scuttled about, now they fed again. They made a sight worth seeing.

"Offended?" Dan asked.

"Not a bit. In my way, and after my fashion, I am wise. Not because I'm particularly intelligent, please understand, but because my business makes me so. Dan, a visiting nurse meets all kinds of people in all kinds of conditions of need. She sees something, and she learns. So perhaps, in the end, all of us who work this way become wiser than our years and even wiser than we should be. Wise, I should add, in the way of life."

"Yet you wouldn't abandon your profession, Miss March, if you weren't well paid."

Dawn's lustrous brunette head described a short nod.

66

"I feel the same way, Miss March."

"Except that you're not carrying your weight. Insofar as the county is concerned, you're an object of charity. Insofar as most of the people in Port West are concerned, you're a nice enough fellow but have to be cared for. There isn't much dignity in that, it seems to me."

He flushed. He glowered at the ocean. "Anyone can make money. I've had offers. I can always have offers."

"Well, then?"

"To do what, though? To paint pretty birds that aren't birds at all? To paint the sea as it never is, but the way some editor thinks it ought to be?"

"Magazine offers?"

He didn't answer. He was looking west now, and apparently saw something that annoyed him. He said almost savagely, "There are ways and ways to earn money, Miss March. Some people don't care how they do it because all they can think of is money. But others? Well, I'll get along. In a few months my debt to the county will be paid. In the meantime . . . well, it would seem I'm to have another visitor."

Dawn looked west over her shoulder, and was unpleasantly surprised. The visitor was Mrs. Clara Royce, and Mrs. Royce was her customary lovely self in a very beautiful pair of slacks and a cashmere sweater. Dawn got up as the woman headed for the sand dune.

Seen against the backdrop of the sea and sky, Mrs. Clara Royce gave the illusion of being small, fragile, and quite helpless. But when she reached the dune all that quite abruptly disappeared. She smiled at Dan, nodded coolly at Dawn. "Well, Mr. Colby," she said cheerfully, "it's delightful to see you again. I have been anxious to have a private chat with you."

A perverse streak in Dawn's nature did the rest. She simply sat down beside Dan, and waited.

The blue eyes of Mrs. Royce showed surprise. She used another stratagem. "Miss March," she asked, "would you mind giving me several minutes with Mr. Colby?"

Dawn began to enjoy herself. "As a matter of fact," she said, "I would mind."

Dan straightened, as if pinched.

A faint, threadlike wrinkle appeared in the lovely forehead of Mrs. Royce. "Oh, dear," she said, "I didn't mean to make an issue of it, Miss March. Actually, all I've come here for is a painting. Mr. Colby, it seems to me that you're greatly talented and that much could be done with your work. I myself think enough of it to offer you a hundred dollars for each painting of a seagull that you own."

Dawn drew a sharp breath. Good heavens, if he were to grab that offer he'd have a thousand dollars to his name, at least!

Dan Colby grinned easily. "What would you do with them, Mrs. Royce?"

"Hold them for a time. Then sell them at a profit, if I could. The usual business arrangement, I believe."

Dan nodded. "I suppose so. But why the sudden interest in my work?"

Dawn waited for the answer to that, as curious as Dan seemed to be.

The answer, when it came, startled her.

"I intend to live in Port West, Mr. Colby. I naturally wish to make a place for myself in the community, and I naturally wish to contribute to the growth of my community. It seems to me that we are very fortunate to have a man of your talent living among us. I propose to hold an exhibition of your work, here in Port West. I have a few Los Angeles press connections and can, I believe, obtain newspaper coverage. You see? I would be doing Port West a service. I would be doing you a service. I would be doing myself a service. The usual business arrangement, as I have said."

It was frightening to Dawn. This was the business mind that Ken had extolled, and now she understood why Ken had fibbed to her that evening things were supposed to be patched up between them. If you were ambitious, and if you listened to a woman like Mrs. Royce . . .

"Oh, I don't know," she heard Dan say, and she swung her mind back to the moment. "You see, Mrs. Royce, I can obtain all the commissions I want. Furthermore, I seldom sell my work."

"Isn't that foolish?"

"I have been told that it's foolish."

"Without money, Mr. Colby, what are you?"

"An artist."

"I see."

And Mrs. Clara Royce stood up. She stood thinking about this refusal she'd received, and it was clear that she had been made unhappy. However, she offered no argument. She simply gave a shrug that could have signified anything, then said good evening and went back down the sand dune to the beach. A few minutes later she was a tiny sight against the backdrop of ocean and sunset sky.

Dawn decided that she ought to go home, too. It had been a pleasant walk, it had been good exercise, but certainly she'd had little opportunity to do any thinking about Ken. And it was vital that she think about Ken. She'd have another evening with him come Friday, and by that time she ought to have a good notion of what she wanted to say to him and why she wanted to say it. Still, she felt reluctant to leave, and so she lingered on the dune with Dan until Wes came at ten to help the artist back to his house within the dump. Afterward, she walked slowly home with Wes.

"You surprised me," Wes said. "I thought you didn't bother with your patients after hours."

"It isn't ever a good idea. But I was so surprised and angry to see him sitting there that—incidentally, don't do it again, Wes, please?"

"A fellow could go crazy cooped up in a place like that."

"Or you could fall, or he could fall, and the damage to the knee might be permanent."

He whistled.

Dawn fell into step beside him. She was reminded of other walks she'd had with Wes along this same strip of beach, and they were pleasant memories that caused her to smile. She took his arm companionably, and when he promptly pecked at her cheek she wasn't annoyed or even troubled. "Be good," she said lazily. "Wes, do you love this old town as much as I love it?"

"I'd like to see it grow, prosper."

"So would I. But I'd not want it to become a roaring metropolis, Wes. It's nicer as it is."

He gave her hand a squeeze, and she had another memory. The night she'd graduated from high school she'd walked with Wes along this beach. Wes had been filled with ideas about marrying her as soon as they could obtain a license. Then she'd had to tell him she'd decided to become a nurse.

He'd stopped short, utterly surprised and deeply hurt. "Don't be foolish," he said. "You'd hate it."

Yet she'd never regretted the decision she'd made, nor would she. It was satisfying to know how to do something, to carry one's own weight. It was good to know, hang it, that she was adequate to cope with life around her and with the problems even others had.

"Did you know," she asked, "that Mrs. Royce really intends to live in Port West?"

"Yes. In fact, I've been showing her houses lately. She wants about five acres already planted in orange trees. And the place must be on a hill, and she must have a view of the ocean. A difficult order to fill, but she seems to have the necessary money. Why did you ask?"

"She's a strange woman, isn't she? I mean, she seems to believe that only she is important."

"Possibly that's how she got ahead. I didn't get the idea when I talked to her that she'd always had money. And I didn't get the idea, either, that she'd acquired her money easily."

No, Dawn reflected, it couldn't have been easy money. What the money represented, actually, was so many shattered illusions and dreams. Pathetic, but that was probably how it was. And now Mrs. Royce had Ken Jones spinning dreams. What would Ken be like if those dreams were shattered, eh?

They reached the foot of the beach and the junction of the beach with Tinsley Way. Wes helped her up the embankment of sand and boulders and ambled along with her to her car.

"Mrs. Royce wants to give Dan an exhibition, Wes."

"I know. She discussed it with me."

"Good idea?"

"Why not? You know, Dawn, I'm beginning to understand why you're fascinated by your work. You see someone who needs help, and it's a satisfaction to provide that help. Well, that's how I feel about Dan. I think if he could be jogged up a bit he'd do a lot."

"Why not send a painting of his to one of the big magazines? Just get an opinion of it—you know, something to show him."

"Why bother?" Wes asked. "Mr. Patton did that a few months ago and the magazine offered to give Dan a commission to paint a series on sea birds. Dan turned it down cold."

Dawn stopped short, astonished. "Really?"

And then, abruptly, she got mad. "And I've been giving him free nursing service? Why, the very idea!"

It was while she was driving home alone, very cross with Dan Colby, that her great and brilliant idea first flitted into her churning mind.

Chapter X

MR. PATTON BLINKED AND SCOWLED. HE PEERED THROUGH
the haze of bluish-gray cigar smoke at the composed Dawn
March and the obviously disquieted Harriette Jones. He
harumphed portentously. The appearance of his wife, however, prevented him from immediately voicing his reaction
to Dawn's suggestion. He struggled to his feet and followed
in his wife's wake across the library to his wife's favorite chair.
He thereupon seated his wife with a nice display of gallantry.
"Comfortable?" he asked. "Not troubled by a draft, are you?"

"Quite comfortable, dear."

It was refreshing to Dawn to see the loving look she gave
him as he doughtily trudged back to his own chair. When
she was married, she thought, it would be like that. She
gave a sentimental smile to Mr. Patton, and resumed.

"Before you explode," she said crisply, "think of it this way.
Your method of helping Dan Colby has been wrong, demon-
strably wrong. In effect, all you have done is make it possible
for him to exist after a fashion and indulge himself to his
heart's content."

"The boy works. Give him credit."

"But only as it suits him to, and when it suits him to. And
he does not learn, and he therefore does not progress, because
the only work he does is the work he chooses to do in the
way he chooses to do it. That isn't the way to develop."

"I notice that you do concede he works. Of course the
boy works. He's done almost a hundred paintings. Grueling
work, you have to concede that, too."

Mr. Floyd Patton seemed awfully pleased with the mere
idea of work. He smiled just before he returned the cigar to
his mouth.

Dawn swung around slightly in her chair to include Mrs.
Patton in the conversation. She was convinced that if Mrs.
Patton were to see her point, the first step in the rehabilitation
of Mr. Dan Colby would be achieved. It was pretty obvious
to anyone who sat in that library that Mr. Patton approved
of whatever his wife approved.

"Growth," she said thoughtfully, "is actually development through progression. A child's mind is developed by exposure to progressively difficult education. On the other hand, a child's mind stagnates if the only lesson you teach him is a lesson he has already learned. My own suspicion is that that's how it is with Dan Colby. He paints but one type of thing, he uses but one technique. Admittedly, he works, and the work he does is effective. The only things wrong with it is that it doesn't sell and he doesn't actually support himself."

She paused to get her breath and to appraise the reaction she was getting from Mrs. Patton. Mrs. Patton's expression told her nothing.

"Yes, sir," Mr. Patton said, "that boy works as you like to see a boy work. No lazy streak in him, all right."

"And what happens," Dawn asked, "if you both die?"

"Die?" Mr. Patton half arose, his face congesting with angry color.

"It happens," Dawn said quietly. "If you worked in my profession, sir—"

"How dare you suggest such a thing?"

Dawn's gaze slid over toward Mrs. Patton on her left. Having achieved the effect she wanted, she now made her second bid for Mrs. Patton's support. "Ma'am," she said intensely, "if he's to be just an object of charity, then your method of helping him is perfectly all right. But if his well-being isn't to be utterly dependent upon the fact of your existence, then your method isn't all right. What would happen if your help were suddenly withdrawn? Surely you can see my point."

Mrs. Patton looked down at her hands, a slim woman with graying auburn hair. She was dressed this afternoon in dull green gabardine slacks and a short-sleeved cocoa-brown cashmere sweater. She wore no jewelry other than her engagement ring and wedding ring, and that amused Dawn, because it was well-known that Mr. Patton was fond of buying "lovely baubles" for his Marcia.

"I think," Mr. Patton rumbled, "that you've overlooked an important point, young lady. You've overlooked the fact that I always know what I'm doing. I don't support anyone in idleness. If I didn't know the boy worked, I'd not give him a penny."

73

"Did you know, sir, that Dan Colby could obtain a number of commissions from important magazines?"

He grinned broadly, almost laughed. "Now there you have it, Dawn. Of course I know about it. I myself sent some of Dan's things east. I was anxious to get a professional opinion of his work. I obtained that opinion, and the offer, and I took it all up with Dan. And the boy was seriously tempted, believe me. He was eager to continue to accept my money. We threshed the whole thing out. In the end we agreed that another year or so would give him the time he needs to develop his ability and to——"

"To what point, sir, is the ability to be developed?"

"Until he's learned what he needs to learn, of course."

It took Dawn aback. This was a business man talking, one of those hard-headed business men who were reputed to measure everything in terms of dollars, success? But how fantastic! And how horrible for Dan!

She stood up, feeling that she'd said all she could say, and that further words would be useless. It was apparent to her now that Mr. Patton fancied himself in the role of a patron of the arts and that he'd continue to patronize Dan Colby for as long as Dan actually did work over and over again on the sort of things he could already do well. She gave Harriette a smile and turned to say her good-byes to Mrs. Patton. But Mrs. Patton, it developed, wasn't quite ready to permit her to leave. "Sit down, dear," she said pleasantly. "It's apparent you disapprove of our method of assisting Dan, and I'm naturally disturbed. According to Miss Grand, you're not a person who talks merely for the sake of talking. Is it your opinion that Dan is too apt to allow others to do his worrying for him?"

"Not really. I simply think he must learn the same things we all must learn—that is, to earn our living while we're also preparing ourselves to do the sort of work we want to do. I'm sorry, ma'am, but I really don't think Dan Colby is a special sort of human being. Nor do I consider him to be a better artist than many artists who are currently being compelled by circumstances to earn their living doing commercial art—all that. And I do think that if Dan Colby can do it, then he owes it to himself and to the community to accept the commissions he's offered and——"

"What does the community have to do with this?" Mr. Patton demanded.

"He's had free medical and nursing care, Mr. Patton. To that degree he's certainly obligated to the county and the community."

"I'll send a check, if that's what troubling you."

"I think you know me well enough to know that isn't what's troubling me. I simply dislike watching well-intentioned people like you turning a person like Dan into a sort of bum. If you really want to help someone who can use all your help, I'll give you a dozen names. And the people I'll name are people who simply cannot work, not people who don't choose to work."

It looked nip and tuck for a moment. Mr. Patton wasn't accustomed to this sort of talk, and it was obvious that he didn't like it. But now the earlier remarks which had actually been aimed at Mrs. Patton began to bear fruit. Mrs. Patton looked up at her standing, furious husband and suddenly asked: "Floyd, why isn't it possible for Dan to do a few things for the magazines? I mean, in what way would the experience be injurious to his career?"

"An artist, a true artist, paints the thing that's important to him. He's the one who determines what is or isn't important. But a commercial hack—"

"May I interrupt?" Dawn asked.

He gave her a savage look, but shrugged.

And Dawn dropped her bombshell. "Mrs. Clara Royce will buy things Dan has already painted, sir. She'll take them to Los Angeles and sell them. There, it seems to me that's a fair proposition. Dan will still be choosing his own subjects, and he'll still be painting the things he wants to paint, the things that are important to him."

"Clara Royce? Who's she?"

It was Mrs. Patton who told him, and it was quite clear that Mrs. Patton shared the general dislike the ladies of Port West seemed to have for the beautiful Mrs. Royce. A few minutes later, when Dawn and Harriette left, Dawn had a strong conviction that she'd at last managed to do Dan some real good. It might take time to bring Mr. Patton to his senses, but surely Mrs. Patton would accomplish it.

She gave Harriette a grin. "It'll march. I have a strong hunch it'll march."

Harriette said nothing. Her lovely face strangely set, she just walked over to Dawn's car and got in.

75

Chapter XI

IN LOS ANGELES, ON A TERRIBLY HOT AND SMOGGY AFTER-
noon, Mrs. Clara Royce stepped into a certain office building
on Wilshire Avenue and gave her name to the pretty redheaded
receptionist behind the imposing lobby desk. The receptionist
looked dubious. "I think Mr. Klaus is out, Mrs. Royce. Are
you certain your appointment was for this afternoon?"

"I had no appointment, miss."

The receptionist smiled, and a certain confidence came
into her manner. "Oh, then in that case, Mrs. Royce, may I
suggest that you write Mr. Klaus, asking for an appointment?
Mr. Klaus has a very full schedule."

"I'm certain, quite certain, that he'll see me."

It was difficult for the receptionist to peg this tall, beautifully dressed, stunning woman before her. The woman had
such an air. Yet she could hardly be a business woman,
because a business woman would have known better than to
try to see Mr. Klaus before she'd made an appointment.

The receptionist solved her dilemma by asking carefully:
"Well, Mrs. Royce, I'll certainly be glad to announce you
to his secretary. Would you mind stating your business,
please?"

The lovely blue eyes twinkled. "Certainly not. Pray inform
Mr. Klaus that I have come here to make money by showing
him how to make money."

The receptionist dialed a telephone number, and eventually
Clara Royce was taken upstairs to a large suite of offices on
the top floor of the ten-storey building. She was shown into
the office of Mr. North who rose and bowed and saw to it that
she was comfortably seated. The eyes of Mr. North roved, as
the eyes of men will, and Clara Royce was considerably
amused. "Oh, yes," she chuckled, "they are my own ankles,
Mr. North. Thank you for admiring them."

He sat down, not at all discomposed. "One never is sure, Mrs. Royce. But one is astonished, if one may state it. Lovely women aren't often interested in business."

"I have always been a strange woman, Mr. North, perhaps because I was so dreadfully poor as a child. I always say there is nothing like poverty to teach one the value of money. Incidentally, I do know the value of money, and I also know the value of the information I possess."

He made a tent of his fingers and peered over that tent solemnly. "And what was this information, Mrs. Royce?"

She smiled ravishingly. "I do wish you were other than a flunkey, Mr. North. I like to be polite. I like to answer questions that are addressed to me. Still . . ."

It scored!

He was baffled by her cockiness, just as the girl downstairs had been, and like the girl he didn't seem to know what to do next. He became, of course, almost obsequiously polite.

"Now I did not intend to pry, Mrs. Royce. But it is my duty to spare Mr. Klaus as many interruptions and distractions as I can. You are aware, of course, that a man of his importance must jealously guard his time?"

"Certainly, Mr. North. And perhaps I should tell you this: I think that the deep, eternal gratitude of the Colby Steel Corporation would be of value to Mr. Klaus. Do you think Mr. Klaus would concur in that opinion?"

His expression told her nothing, but Clara Royce hadn't anticipated that it would. Mr. Klaus had the reputation of picking good men, and a man in the position of Mr. North would hardly be a bungling dunderhead. Very matter-of-factly he said: "I'm sure I wouldn't know, Mrs. Royce. What did you expect to gain, shall we say, from assisting Mr. Klaus to put the Colby Steel Corporation under an obligation to him?"

"Perhaps an expression of interest in a certain tract of land. Nothing more would be required."

He got it, and whistled. "I see. Land values would rise, you would sell certain holdings adjoining that land, and make a killing."

"I do adore to make killings," Clara Royce admitted. "As I have said, I am intensely aware of the value of money."

He shook his head firmly. "Unfortunately, Mrs. Royce, we don't do business that way. It wouldn't help our reputation."

77

Clara Royce sighed, but said little more. "Oh, I see. Then I do apologize. Mr. North, for having wasted your time. It was quite silly of me, but I did hope, and—well, no matter. Will you tell me how to get back to the Michel Hotel in Beverly Hills, please?"

"I'm sure," he said gently, "that any taxi driver will know the way, Mrs. Royce. Good afternoon."

Clara Royce cabbed back to the hotel. She went directly to her room on the eleventh floor and changed into a cool negligee and stretched out on the comfortable bed to do some thinking. So far, she concluded, she'd make excellent progress. She had made the contact, and had actually met a much more important person than she'd expected to meet at this point in the proceedings. In that very fact, it pleased her to think, was a strong indication she'd chosen the right firm with which to do business. She'd not have won such quick and easy entry into the office of Mr. North had the Klaus organization not been interested in new opportunities to make money. She must not be too optimistic, however. Only Mr. Klaus himself could determine the value a good connection with the Colby Steel Corporation would have for his firm. Then, and only then, would there be some justification for optimism. In the meantime, perhaps she ought to arrange for competition. A strong competitive position might be useful if and when she actually faced Mr. Klaus to arrange the terms.

Clara Royce gave considerable thought to this matter. Her first inclination was to telephone Harold, but she soon found several good reasons for trying to think of someone else. Harold would be suspected of working in collusion with her, inasmuch as they'd once been man and wife. Then there was the fact that Harold could be a devil when he chose to be. He would probably choose to be, because it went against his grain to be defeated, and she'd badly defeated him before he'd ever realized they were actually locked in combat. It would be typical of Harold to go to Port West, tell what he knew, and arrange for her to take a heavy financial loss. Once she'd taken the loss, he would of course be tardy in his alimony payments to press her even flatter against the wall. He would then offer a deal calling for a lower monthly alimony payment than she now received, and how could she refuse to accept the lower payments? It would be accept them,

78

or fight, and where would she find the money necessary to battle him through all the courts of California?

Clara Royce smiled tightly in the privacy of her room, and it wasn't a pretty smile. No, no, she told herself, Harold wasn't the person to go to now. But perhaps her third husband? Poor fellow, he was still so terribly, terribly in love!

Clara Royce sat up quickly, excitement blazing in her eyes. On an impulse, she darted to the telephone table across the room and put in a call to the Coggins Department Store. She got through to Leroy with a minimum of fuss and was delighted by the tone that at once came into his voice. It was such a shame, she mused, that he was such a terribly dull old man. He would always treasure the memory he had of her, and under other circumstances marriage would be quite convenient.

"I've missed you," Leroy said honestly. "I've wondered where you were."

"Here, there, everywhere. So much to see, darling, and so little time in which to see it."

"You must settle down," he said worriedly. "Clara, you must find an interest, a niche, and settle down."

"I know, I know. And I'm always promising myself that one day I'll do so. But you know me, Leroy. Are you busy?"

The answer was long in coming. Then a defensive note came into his voice as he said: "Well, as a matter of fact, I am. And I may as well tell you now, Clara, that I have decided to restore order to my life. The woman lacks your beauty, of course, but she seems to be interested in the life I can give her."

"Oh? Do I know her?"

"No, you don't know her. A woman I met while in New York last week. We had dinner every night, and it was—well, agreeable."

It galled Clara Royce to think that he, of all people, could in effect turn her down now. She snapped: "I see, Leroy. Well, may I make a suggestion? Try to stop being such a terribly dull old creature, will you?"

"Now that isn't nice, Clara. I did my best, and you know it. We went here, there, everywhere. My business suffered. It became necessary to see to the business. You know that."

Clara Royce slammed the handset to the standard. So much for Leroy. If he were involved in another love affair he'd be quite useless to her. He'd be certain to tell the other woman, and it was quite likely the other woman would intervene. No. Better to go it alone, without the strength of a competitive position, than to give anyone the chance to do her an injury at the last minute. And perhaps she didn't require additional strength. Well, enough of this pointless stewing. She was in Los Angeles! Evening was coming on! She was young, beautiful, she had plenty of money! Why not dress, go to some good restaurant for dinner, go to some good night club afterward to see a show? What would be, would be. And who could say that she'd not do herself some good somewhere along the line this evening? Men were such silly creatures, so vulnerable. Consider Ken Jones in Port West. Consider Wes Overton in Port West. Consider the men she'd married to advantage. Weren't other men around?

It was while Clara Royce was dressing that the knock sounded softly on her door. She opened it a crack, puzzled, then gave a little laugh to allow the pretty redhead to enter. "You're the Klaus receptionist, aren't you? Well, how nice to see you, dear. Care for a drink?"

"Golly, no, Mrs. Royce—not during working hours."

Clara closed the door, waved the girl to a chair. She was interested to notice that the girl was considerably impressed by the appearance of the room, and she inevitably wondered if the girl knew the value of money. "Mr. Klaus, I take it, is interested in seeing me, miss?"

"Helene Liken, Mrs. Royce. Goodness, but this is a beautiful room, isn't it?"

"Quite satisfactory. The windows offer a grand view of the city. Why don't you enjoy the view while I finish dressing?"

The girl grinned and hustled to one of the windows. Clara kept her standing there a long time, in no hurry to get on with the task. Only when it suited her did she call out and wave the girl back to a chair. Dressed now in an afternoon frock of Italian silk, she took an armchair near the wall and frankly appraised the girl's face. A bit innocent, she decided, but certainly interested in clothes, in a show of luxury, and therefore vulnerable. "Well," she asked, "what did Mr. Klaus tell you to ask me?"

"Mr. North wondered, Mrs. Royce, if you would like dinner at the Castle this evening."

"I doubt it. I'm afraid, dear, that I like to eat my meals alone. Men are inclined to talk business at table, have you noticed? I find that interferes with the pleasure I take in my food. Did you drop a hundred dollars as you entered?"

The redhead gasped.

Clara Royce extracted a hundred-dollar bill from her handbag. "I picked it from the floor, dear. I wonder why Mr. North wishes to take me to dinner."

It was pathetic, really. The girl was so obviously interested in the hundred-dollar bill, and yet she did possess a certain loyalty to her employer. The sense of loyalty triumphed. "I guess," Helene Liken sighed, "that I didn't drop that money after all. I'm to tell you that Mr. North will be at the Castle at eight o'clock."

"I won't be, thank you."

Nor did Clara change her mind. Instead, she ate a lonely, dull dinner in the restaurant of the hotel, and after dinner she went to a motion picture and sat through the double bill twice. She was convinced she was paying a terribly high price for the luxury of seeming quite independent and sure of herself, but when she returned to the hotel and found Mr. North waiting in the lobby she decided that her stratagem had paid off.

"My," she exclaimed, "such a surprise, sir."

"Shall we take a walk?"

"How far?"

"To a limousine in the hotel parking lot?"

Clara's heart drummed. She said huskily, "It is important to your firm, isn't it? Oh, I won't raise my price, Mr. North. I never play it that way."

He said nothing. His hand tightly gripping her arm, he led her along a back hall to the exit to the parking lot. He ushered her into the limousine, made the introduction, and discreetly withdrew. After a moment of silence the hulking man on the rear seat asked: "How firm an interest in a certain tract of land would you require, Mrs. Royce?"

"An option to buy would serve. I myself would provide the five thousand dollars that would probably be involved. Notice, Mr. Klaus, that actually the proposition will cost you nothing?"

"You have intelligence, Mrs. Royce. You interest me. Precisely what have you in mind?"

"I have an option on all the wasteland surrounding the tract of land you might wish to purchase for industrial reasons. I wish, presumably, to create a beach estate. Still, if I were offered a fair profit I could be persuaded to sell out. I would probably net fifty or sixty thousand dollars."

"You obviously know where the boy is. How did you find out?"

Clara laughed softly. "I go here, there, everywhere, Mr. Klaus. Call me a wretched creature with a passion for excitement, adventure. Still, that's how I am. I met a fellow in New York in Greenwich Village, who knew a great secret, sir. He knew, in short, the address of Mr. Daniel E. Colby—and in time, I knew the address, too."

"Where is he?"

"In Port West—a rather dismal community fifty miles north, on the coast. Mr. Daniel E. Colby is now the proprietor of the community dump, and he does paint very magnificent pictures."

He grunted.

After a ten second silence he asked: "Now, then, Mrs. Royce, why shouldn't I make use of the information without paying you your fee?"

Clara had the answer to that one, though. With a croon in her voice she asked: "Now aren't you really too big for that sort of thing, sir?"

He agreed. Men always did, she was amused to think, when you'd buttered up their vanity.

After they'd shaken hands on it, he suggested dinner, and Clara didn't refuse. A girl could always toy with the food, she was experienced enough to realize, while a vain man bragged and in the act gave her useful information. . . .

Chapter XII

Dawn's official connection with the Dan Colby case was terminated toward the end of May by a briefly worded memo from Nellie Grand. In turn, she wrote a brief report for the records, turned it in to Mrs. Berry, accepted several other assignments in the squalid Mexican quarter of Oxton, and proceeded to forget that Dan Colby existed. She hoped that he would become the artist he was convinced he'd be, and she further hoped that the Pattons would think seriously about the matter before they sent him another check to cover his basic expenses for June. She then closed her books on Dan Colby and paid a visit to Sammy Berman's office in Oxton. She caught the long, lean, red-headed lawyer studying at his desk. He gave her a quick, friendly grin, and waved her to a chair. "Hail," he said. "I know you're no ghost because your cheeks are much too flushed."

Dawn took the chair, grinning. This was one of her favorite persons. This was a fellow who slugged it out the hard way, a fellow who brooked no interference from anyone, and who refused to allow circumstances to get in his way. So he was an important lawyer in the Oxton-Port West community, and in time, she was positive, he'd be one of their county judges. "Any news?" she asked.

His green eyes became stabbing little daggers. "What did you know about the Dover affair?"

"Nothing."

"If you weren't Dawn March I'd call you a liar. Everyone was convinced of his guilt. So was I. I took him on only because I knew you'd not give me any peace if I refused. Okay. Then I go to the bank and ask innumerable questions, and presently I'm not entirely convinced of the man's guilt. It doesn't add up to a logical crime, you see. Dover is no fool. He surely would have taken certain steps to prevent suspicion from falling on him. The way it was done, however —well, suspicion was bound to fall on him first."

"Then I doubt he is guilty. Mr. Dover is pretty intelligent, Sammy."

Sammy got restlessly from his chair. He took off his jacket, loosed his collar, paced over to the window for some fresh air. He stood gazing out at the Oxton scene, his lips a tight line, his body held rigidly, straightly. "Any suspicions?" he asked.

Dawn grinned faintly. "I'm sorry to disillusion you, Sammy, but I'm really not psychic."

He turned, shrugged. "Look, Dawn, shall we stop fencing with one another? I know how you work. You go into mean little houses to help people in desperate circumstances. You walk in as you are now, spick and span from head to toe, smelling of a nice perfume, a smile on your face, sympathy in your eyes, and help and comfort in your mind, your hands. In a crisis, you're there, and so sweetly they're bound to love you, trust you—and talk."

Dawn shook her head.

Sammy wasn't to be shaken that easily. "They talk because they're human beings in trouble and because human beings in trouble have to talk. I'd like to worm my way into that noggin of yours. Ah, the secrets of this community that I'd know!"

"No talk, Sammy. I wouldn't fib."

"Not if I were to ask a direct question. There's the rub, however. I don't know the right questions to ask. I could try, of course. For instance, did anyone tell you that on the night the crime was presumably committed Mr. Dover was over in the Mexican quarter looking for a gardener he used to employ?"

They were interrupted by Sammy's secretary. Sammy took the message, nodded, said he'd telephone Mrs. Clara Royce later in the afternoon. He was excited by the message his secretary had handed him, and Dawn wondered why. "Don't tell me," she probed, "that Mrs. Royce has decided to buy a place after all?"

"Many places, Dawn. I wish I knew something. I wish I understood why Mrs. Royce is very quietly obtaining options to buy acre after acre over toward your Port West dump. She did mention something to the effect that she hopes to acquire a beach estate—but is that logical?"

Dawn wrinkled her forehead dutifully and gave it a fraction of a second's thought. "I wouldn't call it it logical," she said, and there dismissed the matter. "I did hear," she said carefully, "that Mr. Dover was in the quarter that night, looking for old Pedro. Why?"

"The crime was committed that evening, Dawn. I can't prove that yet, but I will. Logically, it had to be committed that night, and early in the night; in the evening, in short. So if Dover was there in the quarter he couldn't possibly be guilty, eh?"

Dawn said nothing, just sat there looking at him and listening.

Sammy smiled crookedly. "I'd not for a moment suggest that you use your official position to help Dover, and I'd not for a moment suggest that you take advantage of anyone in desperate circumstances to—well, ask a few questions. Still, it would be very helpful to know the exact time Dover went to the quarter, and the exact time he left it."

Dawn stood up, looking at her watch. "Time is a peculiar thing, Sammy. In the quarter, for instance, about an hour can mean any period of time from one minute to three or four hours. Still, if I ever do learn the answer to that question, I'll give it to you. How is he bearing up under all this?"

"Why not go see for yourself?"

"He's a very nice man, Sammy. Very proud, though. And sometimes it's kind not to visit people during moments of stress. Furthermore, I'm busy."

He walked over to her, grinning, and gave her a mock punch on the chin. "You softie," he said. "You're much too soft for your own good. How's the romance progressing?"

"Oh, I still see Ken."

He grimaced. "I meant the genuine article. To me, that means Wes Overton. Stop being an idiot, Dawn, and grab your guy while you can have him."

Dawn left, quite exasperated. She wished that her friends would kindly stop banging away on that same old theme that she had to love Wes because she'd always loved Wes. In the first place, she hadn't always loved Wes. In the second place, there were loves and loves—the love you had for a friend, the love you had for a brother, the love you had for the man you hoped to marry. And in the third place, hang it, she did love Ken. He suited her. He suited her in just about every respect. True, he'd been bitten by the ambition bug recently, but that would pass. The real Ken was the fellow

85

who gave ten and twelve hours a week to the free dental clinics in the area. They talked the same language, basically, and they had the same aspirations to live in Port West, serve their community, and fulfill their destinies both as human beings and as professional people. Whereas what did she have in common with Wes?

She drove back to the Mexican quarter and parked her car before the La Stella Grocery Store. She got her kit slung from her shoulder and stepped down from the car to pick her way through the side alley that led to a longer, broader alley at the rear. It was a scorcher of an alley that afternoon, all right, and it seemed to her that every cat and dog in the quarter was lying in the alley trying to get a breath of air. None so much as bared a tooth at her, and she didn't blame them. She wanted to lie down herself and do just some plain everyday breathing, too. The quarter was a disgrace, she thought. Look at the ramshackle houses human beings were supposed to live in. Florence Street in Port West was horrible enough, but this—

Sighing, she found the little green shack she was seeking and gave the door a perfunctory knock. In the little room beyond the door she found Mrs. Gomez sitting as one stupefied in a rocking chair. "Hi," she called to the old lady. "Cold enough for you?"

Mrs. Gomez wearily smiled. "Some day when I die," she said, "I'm gonna laugh at the flames down below. They ain't got nothin' on what I'm sufferin' right now."

Dawn half lifted her from the chair and half carried her over to the bed. She got the woman stretched out prone, then opened the back of her damp cotton dress. She removed the dressing from the wound and studied the raw, infected flesh. Little progress, she saw, and she quite understood it. "You scratch too much, Mrs. Gomez. That doesn't help. You'll have serious trouble if you don't keep your nails away from this wound."

"When I itch, I scratch. I just do it. Ain't it coming along, Miss March?"

Dawn methodically got her things from the kit and cleaned and dressed the wound. "You'll live," she said dryly. "I never lose patients in the quarter, did you know?"

86

"We're tough, Miss March. Around here we gotta be. I talked to the insurance man. He says I ain't got much of a case."

"You slipped and fell through that showcase, didn't you? Of course you have a case."

"He says fifty dollars is all the case I got."

"Tell him you want a thousand, and settle for five hundred."

Mrs. Gomez laughed. "For five hundred I'll fall through that showcase again."

Dawn buttoned the dress and helped Mrs. Gomez back to the rocker. She put her equipment away and bustled about cleaning up the room. "Any news that's interesting?" she asked.

Mrs. Gomez shrugged. "You know Tony who got in trouble stealing cars?"

"Yes."

"The wife is gonna have a baby. A real fine baby, only Tony, he ain't gonna be where he can see that baby. The priest, he says he'll do what he can, only what can a priest do?"

"That is a shame."

"You know Josephine? Well, her store is making out. I guess she's got a real fine head for making money, that Josephine."

Reminded, Dawn wondered if she should take the time to give Josephine a fair chance at her hair. The crop of hair was becoming too thick. Anyway, she was tired of the old hairdo. What about just pin feathers, for variety?

"You know Manuel?" Mrs. Gomez asked. "The boy has a pretty good job. This rich lady over in Port West, this very beautiful lady, she's got Manuel and his car hired for maybe two, three months, and all the time now they're driving around and she's talking to people who own land over near the dump. Manuel says she's making deals for that land right and left, that rich lady is."

And, Dawn imagined, Sammy Berman's part in the strange business was to check land titles and arrange the legal matters in such a way that the options to buy would be binding anywhere in the courts of California. Her scalp tingled. Recalling what Ken had said about Mrs. Royce's business ability, she began to wonder excitedly what was up. Did Dan Colby know? He knew just about everyone, no doubt, who owned land in that area. And come to think of it, had Mrs. Royce actually visited Dan that evening to discuss buying all the paintings he possessed?

The questions grew in her mind, and that evening she did some blunt probing into the mind of Dr. Ken Jones. Ken was quite disinterested, at first, in any conversation that even remotely involved the beauteous Clara Royce. But the nature of Dawn's questions, and her very obvious excitement, had their effect on Ken. He leaned forward in his chair and rested his forearms on the small, white-clothed table. "So she's buying land, or options, is she? But why in that dreary corner of town, will you answer that?"

"Presumably for a beach estate."

Ken hooted derisively, and Dawn agreed with that sentiment. "Something bigger," he snapped. "A few miles up the coast she could pick up fine acreage for about half the price she'd have to pay here. Mrs. Royce isn't the sort of person who wouldn't know that. I sometimes think she knows too many things."

"At any rate," Dawn said simply, "I'm glad she's dropped that chain-store approach to dentistry. I was afraid she'd persuade you to think it was a good idea."

His gray eyes narrowed. "To be equally honest, Dawn, most of it was my idea. And don't be too sure she's dropped it. I think she likes money as well as I like money. And speaking of money, let's have a chat with Wes, shall we? Is there something afoot we know nothing of? Bad. I have a few thousand to spare. If she's about to make a killing in land—well, I'd like to pick up a few bucks myself."

And the date ended there. Ken refused to be talked out of it. He got her into his car and drove her to Wes Overton's brown-shingled house over in the Port West harbor district. He was as well posted on the habits of Wes Overton, it developed, as she was. He crossed the road and hustled through the dusk toward the fishing pier attached to the big freighter pier. Ten minutes, and there they were in the dusk, Wes carrying a pole over his shoulder and protesting he wanted to catch jack smelts, not talk about business. In time, however, they were in the living-room of the brown-shingled house, with a big map of Port West spread across the floor and the two men studying the parcels of land surrounding the community dump. Dawn had to grin. Had any girl ever played second fiddle to such a dull map before? She sat down and studied the living-room while the two men played at being business tycoons. The living-room surprised her. Wes had bought another armchair of Danish design, and he'd also bought a large ebony-finished lamp table with a striking white marble top. No lamp adorned the lamp table as yet, and Dawn wondered idly what sort of lamp Wes had in mind. She gave him a curious glance, but hurriedly averted her gaze when she discovered that his reddish-brown eyes were curiously studying her. Wes answered her unasked question. "Have you seen some of those glass pieces they're manufacturing in Arkansas, Dawn? Well, the lamp I have in mind is one of those flared bottle affairs with a shade about as large as a snare drum. Then it'll be the long, long haul to buy that couch I told you about."

Ken looked up impatiently. "Let it die, will you? What I want to know is this: is there any land in this dump area that could be used by an industrial organization, say?"

Wes jabbed with his forefinger, described a large circle. "About fifty acres here—held by some insurance company in Los Angeles. It wouldn't add up, however. We'd have heard about it if anyone wanted to plunk a factory down there."

"How would you hear about it?"

"You just don't plunk a factory down where you want to, chum. You need a lot from a community before you can do that. You have to discuss it with the town and county commissioners for one thing, to get their permission. And then—"

"Blah." Ken, very excited now, leaped to his feet. Greed flashed in the gray eyes, greed and a sort of anger that startled Dawn and left her feeling strange. "Look, lunkhead," Ken roared, "I know something about the way that woman thinks. She married twice, played both husbands for suckers, and ended up with big property settlements and big monthly alimony payments. And there are a few other things I could tell you about her. She doesn't make a move with her money until she's eliminated just about every risk you can name. I say she's cornering that land because she's found out that someone *is* going to put a factory there. And me, I want in. How much can you grab for me, and you'd better work fast."

Wes stood up, wagging his curly brown head. "Nuts. If she really knows something she has the land cornered by now.

But I still think she doesn't know anything, that she's trying to create a cheap estate."

Ken swung around and headed for the door. He stopped short, however, and a silly expression came onto his face. The next instant, though, he was moving forward briskly, his right hand outstretched. "Well, Clara," he said jovially, "fancy meeting you here."

"Dear Ken, what a pleasant surprise. But you must never shout, you know, particularly when a front door is standing open." Laughing pleasantly, poised as always, Clara Royce stepped into Wes' living-room. She gave the big, ruggedly handsome fellow a cheery nod, and calmly took a chair. She reached out with a dainty foot and tapped the spread-out map with the toe of her shoe. "My," she said, "has my interest in land interested you, too, Mr. Overton?"

"Ken Jones, Mrs. Royce. I know that land, you see."

"Oh, then you know the fifty acres I'd like to buy? I doubt I can obtain it now, of course, but still—"

The next thing that happened left Dawn dumbfounded. Ken, without a single glance in her direction, took Clara Royce by the hand and hauled her up from the chair. "Beautiful woman," Ken said grimly, "it's time that you and I had a talk."

"The sort of talk I'm interested in, Ken?"

"Look—"

"Do you or don't you stop tormenting this poor, wretched nurse?"

Dawn drew a deep breath.

Ken never noticed that, either. "Well," he countered, "let's put it this way, Clara. You stop leading me on, and I'll stop leading her on. Fair enough?"

Clara Royce gave a quick glance over her shoulder. Was there pity in her lovely blue eyes? Dawn couldn't tell. Then with a soft, self-satisfied chuckle, Clara Royce pushed on ahead of Ken and led him out into the late May evening.

Chapter XIII

Nor did Dawn see Ken again until early July. He was always busy when she buried her pride and paid a visit to Hattie in the green-stuccoed house in Maricopa Street. "And I do mean that he is busy," Hattie told her the fifth evening Dawn rang the Jones' door chimes. "Stop glowering! I love you like a sister even if you did play that mean trick on Dan Colby. But there's a limit to what I can do. He doesn't even talk to me much any more. It's business, business, business. They're working out plans for opening an office in Oxton and another office in Santa Anastasia."

"I'd like to see him, Hattie."

"He isn't here. Oh, come in, if you doubt me. He hasn't been here since Sunday. Darn it, why did that woman come to Port West anyway?"

Dawn turned, her face stony, and began the thousand-mile walk to her car. Her mind caught up with something that Hattie had said, however, and she swung about to study the pert, lovely blonde. "What mean trick did I ever play on Dan Colby?"

"Mr. Patton told him last month that he'd helped him all he could."

Dawn wet her lips.

Hattie came along the walk, took her by the arm, and led her across the road to the beach. She said gently, "You meant well, I know, Dawn. But just between you and me, did you have any logical right to break that up for Dan?"

"If you don't like people, Hattie, it's quite easy to let them go to pot in their own way. It requires no effort, you see. You simply ignore their follies, their mistakes, tell yourself it's none of your business, and forget them. Only I can't do that. Hattie. Good Lord, it isn't because I'm nice, or so sympathetic, or so dedicated to suffering humanity. It's simply that—well, listen, Hattie. Why do poor devils like Dan Colby need me in the first place?"

"Because they're ill or injured, of course."

"Partly, yes. But the big reason they need the services of a county visiting nurse is that they've made so many mistakes, or had such rotten luck, that they lack the money to pay for the services of doctors and nurses. So what good does it do just to help them recover from their injuries, their illnesses? Their real trouble is—well, Dan's trouble is that he had the courage to make a break, to try to paint, but that at the time when he should have kept going he began to kid himself he was getting ahead just fine."

A big wave rolled in, formed a shimmering green wall crested by cream, then toppled, splintered, and crashed. Sanderlings feeding along the wet sand just above the normal water line had to skitter back toward the beach in a hurry. Perhaps a thousand yards out, a freighter stood darkly limned against the horizon.

"What's he doing?" Dawn asked.

Hattie flushed. Hattie scooped a handful of sand from the beach and allowed it to trickle through her fingers. "Am I supposed to know?"

"People talk, Hattie. You've been seeing him from time to time."

"Well, if a fellow's all alone he—well, he does need a decent meal now and again. And stop looking at me that way, too! It was quite accidental. I just happened to have a roast I couldn't eat alone, and Ken was traipsing around heaven knows where and—well, was I supposed to throw that perfectly good roast out?"

Dawn smiled faintly, somewhat wistfully. Now there was the woman she ought to be! The direct approach with something no intelligent man living alone and cooking for himself could refuse. "I'm not criticizing you or even kidding you, Hattie. Actually, my only concern is that he use his intelligence and his ability to earn a decent living for himself. I'd hate to think I spent weeks on his knee just to make him a bum again."

"He's pretty angry with you, I'll tell you that. Do you know what he asked me? He asked if you thought you were God."

But Dawn had heard that before and wasn't discomfited. "They always do," she said quietly. "But the anger passes away, and in their need to support themselves they actually

92

do much better than they ever thought they would. Why not send some of his paintings to one of the outdoors magazines?"

"Dawn?"

"Hattie?"

"He's very nice, Dawn, or isn't he?"

"Quite nice." And Dawn meant that. There'd been intense pain, but Dan Colby had never whimpered. There'd been intense frustration, but Dan Colby had never complained. There'd been acute worry, but Dan Colby had never whined. "As a matter of fact," she added, "I seldom trouble to help people I don't respect. Did Ken say when he'd return?"

"Dawn?"

"Hattie?"

"If I could change things, Dawn, I would. Do you know that? It's something I've wanted for Ken and you for months. But something happens, Dawn, and what can a girl do? I know the Clara Royce type. It doesn't take experience to recognize her type because her type—well, they're found in every age, aren't they, and in every level of society. But again, what can a girl do? Ken is greedy for success and I can't talk to him. And it isn't as if she isn't trying to help him. Why, just last week—well, she sold some of her land options to him, and she's talking of putting that money right back into one of the offices he wants to open. He's getting ahead, doing what he wants to do, and—"

"He doesn't love me, isn't that it?"

"Dawn, it's more than that." And now Hattie's voice became breathy with emotion. "Dawn, it's her, too. I mean, she just steps into the house and Ken comes alive. He laughs and bounces around and they josh one another and—well, what can a friend of yours, and Ken's sister, too, do about that?"

Nothing, Dawn thought, and a few minutes later she drove back to her father's house and stepped gloomily into the living-room. Wes, as always, was parked on the couch, arguing with her father, and very obviously waiting for her. He stood up, grinned. "Pop," he rumbled, "you stopped making sense an hour ago. You're just another old-fashioned country doctor who's lost once he gets away from the one subject he knows."

The pink face of Dr. Roger March turned red. "Young man," he snapped, "it's you who don't make sense. I tell you, the talk is in the air, and it's everywhere. Several patients of mine discussed the project today. Their stories jibed. As I understand it, the Hans Klaus organization in Los Angeles is definitely interested in purchasing fifty acres of land in that vicinity."

Dawn sat down in her usual armchair, feeling too tired and drained to go up to her room to do more fruitless thinking about the smash-up of her romance with Ken Jones. She sat there, her brown eyes dull, looking first at Wes, then at her father. It was odd, she thought, how her father had always backed the wrong fellow. Wes, the fellow who was never going to amount to a hill of beans, had always had loyalty, at least.

"And I think," her father said, his voice crackling, "that you're missing the boat, Wes. Here you are in the real estate business, and do you take advantage of the natural opportunities you have?"

"Why should I," Wes grinned, "when there are always suckers like you itching to buy worthless land?"

"Worthless? I tried to buy an acre out there this morning. Do you know what the asking price was? Fifteen hundred dollars. It took me two solid hours to beat that price down to eleven hundred."

Wes sat down. Now his expression changed. "You bought?"

"Of course I bought."

"From whom?"

"Clara Royce, of course. I tell you, you've allowed her to get ahead of you. The instant you heard she was buying up options you should have swung into action. Good Lord, doesn't it add up? Why would a woman of her position come to Port West in the first place? This is a dull seacoast town, with no social life to speak of. She could have found better swimming and boating elsewhere, too. Yet here she came, and here she stayed and—"

"I'll bet you ten cents, sir, that no factory is ever established in that area."

Dr. Roger March gave a grunt of disgust and just rose and walked out. A minute later the door of his office was slammed shut up the hall. The living-room suddenly was very quiet.

Wes settled back on the couch, crossed his legs, and smiled. "I know a place where they serve nice steak dinners."

"Not tonight, Wes, please."

"Tonight especially, Dawn. I think you're beautiful. But more than that, I think you've hung around this place, moping, long enough. Look, let's say your infatuation ran deep, although I personally doubt it. But what good does moping do?"

No reply. Dawn rested her head against the back of the chair and wearily closed her eyes. The lamplight streaming onto her face brought out sharply the tension she was under. Wes had never known that her mouth could be compressed into so thin and taut a line, nor had he ever known she could look so angrily helpless.

"Too bad," he said wistfully, "that I couldn't spare you the shock. I wish I could have done that."

Her lashes fluttered, but she didn't open her eyes.

In the circumstances, Wes obeyed his natural impulse to go to her chair and sit down on an arm of it. He reached out, gave her head a gentle fondling. "I think," he said firmly, "that I'd be a lucky guy to have you, Dawn. And I think others in town would say the same thing. It's tough, when an infatuation runs deep. I know what I'm talking about, incidentally."

The brown eyes opened.

"No," he growled. "I love you. That isn't infatuation. The infatuation troubled me long before I met you. I was ten or eleven, and—"

"Stop just talking," she pleaded. "Wes, what does he see in her? I'm curious. Before she came along—well, I thought we believed in the same things, dreamed the same dreams, all that."

"She can be exciting," Wes said quickly. "Not because of her physical beauty, although she has that, Lord knows. It's something more. I think that in a peculiar sort of way she epitomizes adventure for Ken. And then, of course, she has confidence and nerve. Quite a potent combination, all in all, if a fellow is tired of being a small-town dentist and hopes to be a success and live it up."

"I thought I knew him, understood him!"

"You didn't."

Her eyes showed hurt. "I'm not that stupid, Wes."

"No. If he'd been one of your patients you'd have been more perceptive. But he wasn't. And he appealed to you. And I imagine it was the old story of not seeing what you didn't want to see. Now, look. In my way I like Ken. I won't

95

talk against him. I think his only fault is that he can't distinguish the genuine from the false. What about that dinner?"

"Not hungry."

"More moping? Your mother's pretty worried about you."

"I'll be all right. Apparently I don't have a chance. Hattie gave me the news this evening. It hurts—but I'll be all right."

He argued for a dinner date that evening, but he didn't actually press the matter, and left a few minutes later once he'd been convinced she simply wasn't in the mood to go anywhere or talk to anyone, even him. But there was neither peace nor an opportunity to think after he'd left. Her father returned to the living-room, sat down, lit a cigar, and very crossly asked: "How long is this nonsense to continue? Talked to Nellie Grand this morning. According to Nellie, you're just a nurse going through the motions of being a nurse."

"If she's dissatisfied, let her hire someone else."

"She could do that, too. You're lucky to work under Nellie. She's a remarkably competent nurse. You'll learn more with her in a year than you'll learn in five years with anyone else."

"Is it important for me to learn?"

"I abhor adults who talk like injured little children. I always long to shoot such."

Dawn thought about going to her room. The mere thought of the effort involved kept her glued to her chair, however.

Dr. March sucked cigar smoke in and let cigar smoke out throught his nose. The gray smoke was only a shade or two lighter than his hair. Curling around his head, the gray smoke gave her the chance to change the subject. "Aren't you smoking too much, Pop?"

"Probably." His cherubic face was unabashed, though. "Did I tell you Mrs. Elliott is a great-grandmother? The great event occurred yesterday afternoon. A boy. A hale and hearty baby boy."

"How wonderful!"

"Other news isn't as pleasant. Dan Colby paid a visit early this afternoon. He looked violent. There were some harsh words to the effect that he'd thank you to mind your own business. Who were you, he wanted to know, to tell his father where he could be found?"

Dawn's mouth dropped open.

In a haze of curling gray cigar smoke, her father's blue eyes registered relief. "That's fine," he said happily. "I thought you had too much sense to do a thing like that—but of late you haven't been yourself."

It worked, although Dawn knew it was all a kind of device to wrench her away from her thoughts involving Ken. She leaned forward curiously. "What else did he say, Pop?"

"Oh, he was furious, all right. But only about that. He did tell me to tell you that he'd sent some paintings to an agent in Los Angeles and that the agent has gotten him a commission to do some seabirds for some movie mogul."

A thrill of delight ran tinglingly down Dawn's legs. "There, I knew he could do something if he'd only try."

"Anyway, his message to you is that he'd thank you to forget his existence."

"Rubbish."

"But convince him of that, if you can. His position is that someone who had access to his cottage—notice how kind I can be—well, this someone, he thinks, got his father's address from his bureau drawer."

Dawn just chuckled. For the first time in a month she began to feel something like her old self. She jumped up animatedly and took a quick step toward the hall door. "Dan knows I'm not a sneak, Pop. You know, the nurse-patient relationship teaches the patient as much about the nurse as the nurse is taught about the patient. Golly, won't Hattie be thrilled?"

"She appeared to be when she was with him this afternoon."

"And she never told me anything about all that? Why, the little traitor!"

Dawn stepped briskly out to the hall. A queer thing happened. A sudden pang of hunger shot through her abdomen, and she suddenly felt weak, all atremble. She turned right rather than left, and invaded the kitchen. She found her mother finishing the dinner dishes and looking somewhat bored and lonely. She marched over to the creature and gave the chubby cheek a kiss. "Hi," she said. "Any leftovers, Ma?"

"I beg your pardon, miss?"

"Food. Chow. Just anything at all will do."

"Have we met, miss?"

"Will you stop teasing a girl—I'm starved!"

That did it, of course. Her mother had never yet been able to resist an outright plea for food. She turned happily from the stove and trudged over to the refrigerator. "Now you just sit down, dear, and tell me all about your woes while I fix you a grand dinner. I'm very glad you decided to eat before you collapsed from hunger. Only last evening I discussed forcible feeding techniques with your father."

"No woes."

Their eyes met, briefly.

Dawn shrugged. "A person is wanted or she isn't, Ma. Or maybe a girl has seen a guy for the first time, who knows? Anyway, life should go on, don't you think?"

"Life always does. Will you have one pork chop or two pork chops?"

Dawn had an inspiration. "I'd better call Wes first. If I know Wes, you'll have to cook a half-dozen."

While her mother stood staring, Dawn loped out to the hall to give the big fellow a ring.

Chapter XIV

FATHER AND SON MET ON THE PORT WEST BEACH ON THE
15th day of July at ten o'clock on a rather cool and foggy
morning. In the distance, the harbor foghorn was blowing
dismally, monotonously, somewhat eerily. The ocean could
scarcely be seen, but it could be heard crashing and booming
in counterbeat to the foghorn. Dan didn't see his father strid-
ing along through the blowing tendrils of fog. Dan was sitting
on a flat-topped rock, his back to the land, his eyes intent
upon the ever-changing scene. This day, for a reason unknown
to him, Dan longed to paint something spooky. He wanted to
paint the head of some fearsome sea-monster emerging from
the fog complete with malignant eyes and flaming breath. It
would be a ridiculous painting, he knew; still, he wanted to
do one.

Thomas Colby saw him, called out. Dan turned, half-rose,
waved his hand. A few moments later, his father seated on
the rock beside him, Dan resumed his study of the gray beach,
the gray fog, and the dominant iron-gray sky. "On a day like
this," he told his father, "California isn't a glorious place to
live."

"The past few days were quite pleasant, Daniel."

"And the tomorrows, or most of them, will be quite pleasant, too. I thought you were en route back to New York."

"It was my intention to be, Daniel. There is business to
transact, and I enjoy transacting business. It would appear,
however, that I am also a sentimental man. Have you ever
read Montaigne?"

Long ago, Dan remembered. But he couldn't recall any of
the essays.

"Montaigne wrote, Daniel, that he had never known a
father to deny his son. Montaigne suggested that this was so
because the boy, for better or worse, belonged to the father.
And then, as I have said, I am a sentimental man."

"How's Mary?"

99

"Enjoying Los Angeles. Sightseeing, celebrity-hunting, that form of nonsense. I believe that yesterday she also purchased a suit. Why do you ask?"

"Isn't it normal to ask about one's sister?"

"I have had good reason, Daniel, for thinking you were not normal in that respect. If I have done you an injustice, I apologize."

Dan turned, the better to see his father's face. His father's expression was impenetrable. Nor did his father betray either his thoughts or emotions in the small ways most men usually did. The hands were quietly folded on the lap. The expensively shod feet were motionless. His father's posture was erect, but not stiffly so.

"What did you expect to accomplish here?" Dan asked curiously. "I've been trying to figure that out ever since you barged in on me several days ago."

His father considered the question, a strange Eastern sight in oxford gray business suit, collar and necktie, and light-weight hat. Then his father said quietly: "I am not in good health, Daniel. I am quite prepared to show you the doctor's report. It may well be that before the end of the year I shall be compelled to step down, deliver the company to the direction of a younger and healthier person."

"What's wrong?"

"No malignancies, no cardiac condition—nothing of that sort. Simply high blood pressure, an ulcer condition—the doctor merely feels that the time has come for—"

"There's a good doctor here. Dr. Roger March. Why don't you allow him to examine you?"

Thomas Colby turned amused blue eyes toward the boy. "I assure you that my doctor is fairly competent, Daniel. He is one of the outstanding doctors in the East."

"Dr. March is outstanding. I'm told he's considered to be one of the most accomplished general practitioners in California. It wouldn't hurt to have him give you an examination."

"The fact is, Daniel, that I have become reconciled to the notion of stepping down. The important thing now is to choose my successor. I once dreamed that you would step into my shoes."

"Listen, Dad . . ."

He was silenced by his father's suddenly upflung hand.

The fog crept in closer to the land. Now the heavy stuff blotted the last of the ocean from view, and overhead the sky seemed to be shrinking. In another half-hour the beach would be lying buried in the fog, and getting home might prove to be somewhat difficult. Still, Dan didn't care. He liked it there on the rocks with his father. He felt in harmony with the fog, the blowing foghorn, the sounding ocean—even with his father.

"I never wanted it this way," he told his father. "I wished to paint, perhaps, but I never would have left as I did if—"

"I spared you a lifetime of grief, Daniel. The woman is wicked, and was always wicked. I think I proved that when I succeeded in buying her off for a mere pittance."

"Or perhaps in her way she loved me, Dad, and still loves me. She's here in Port West, you know, two husbands later, and from time to time she wanders to my establishment in the dump, presumably to buy one of my paintings. She's lovelier now than she was then. You should see Clara now."

"I have seen her. In fact, I entertained her at dinner in Los Angeles last evening. I disagree with your statement that she is lovelier, and I shall continue to think she took advantage of your youth, your inexperience, your—well, your quixotic temperament."

"You should have allowed me to handle it, Dad. You didn't, the whole thing hurt, I left. I suggest this, Dad; that had you been forcibly separated from my mother you, too, would have felt hurt."

Thomas Colby pursed his lips. He stood up, apparently feeling the chill of the fog, and turned to look at the dump. "Is she here to marry you again, Daniel?"

"Yes."

"And you? What is your opinion of her now?"

"She isn't the Clara I married. Too many husbands, too many triumphs, too many self-indulgences. Who knows, you may be partly responsible for all that. It's difficult to believe, but perhaps Clara was hurt, too."

"She was smiling contentedly, Daniel, when the bank cashed my check for one hundred thousand dollars."

Dan jumped, as if stung, from the rock. "You call that a mere pittance?"

"I would have paid her more," his father said calmly. "No matter. Shall I come to the point of my visit? I shall require your services in New York not later than September 1st if I am to step down, in the end, in your favor."

"Maury Klippstein's a good man."

"I am aware of that, Daniel. And I shall not again offer you the opportunity. There, I believe I have said everything necessary."

"I wish you'd see Dr. March, sir."

His father was bitterly amused. "Isn't it rather late Daniel, for you to experience any concern for my health?"

Dan could say nothing in answer to that. Nor could he bring himself to the point of walking back along the beach with his father to the place where his father had parked his rented car. Dan simply stood there watching until his father disappeared into the fog; then he turned right and ambled across the sand to the dump. He wasn't surprised to see Clara sitting in her car, waiting for him. Of late her visits had become a habit.

"Hello," she said happily. "All the hobgoblins defeated, all the dragons slain."

"Hi, Clara. How come you're taking time off from making money?"

"It's a luxury I can afford." She stepped down gracefully from the car and tagged along after him into the house. She shivered. "This is a dreadful barn, darling, haven't you guessed?"

"Recall the tenement flat near the East River?"

She laughed a gay, tinkling laugh that told him she'd long ago forgotten the hatred she'd had for that flat. "Ah, we were younger and happier then, Danny boy, weren't we?"

He lighted the small gas heater, carefully put the match into an ashtray, and turned and studied the appearance she made in gray flannel slacks and a blue cashmere sweater. And it was a queer thing to him that she was still as lovely in his eyes as she'd been that day years ago when they'd sneaked off to West Virginia to be married. Another queer thing was the fact that the mere sight of her here, there, anywhere, could still make his heart bang and his nerves tingle and his stomach quiver with nervous excitement. Breathing hard, he went to an old armchair he'd salvaged from the dump and sat down testily.

102

"You shouldn't be here," he told her. "This isn't New York, and people don't know we've been married. It does you no good and it does me no good."

"What did the old boy want?"

"The same old thing," Dan said wearily. "I pitied him, though. There he sat, pretending to be a hard-headed businessman, come to give me a break I didn't deserve. He sat so close, however, I could have touched him. And had I touched him I think he'd have been the happiest hard-headed businessman in the world."

"But you didn't?"

Her voice, harshly biting, flicked at his eardrums like a whip.

She came across the room, tucked her legs under her and sat back on them. "You're an idiot, Danny boy. For a couple of reasons, if you want to know. First, you still love me. I could be bought off, I could marry two others, I could do anything and everything to disgust and offend you—yet you still love me. And because of that, here you sit. It isn't painting, don't ever think so. It's Danny boy, still hurt, still terribly disillusioned, hiding in a hole so no one can ever see him in his embarrassment and shame."

His jaws hardened.

"Marry the blonde or the brunette, Danny. Or find some hag and marry her. You need a nurse or a fool or a grandmother. Or why not shoot yourself? Or why not brew me some coffee?"

"Why are you here, Clara?"

"To make money."

"Or so you'd like me to think. By the way, what's all the hoopla about the land around here that you've started?"

She giggled, but didn't answer. She got up, and with a lilt in her step hustled to his small kitchen to make the coffee. When she returned her face wore a pink, happy flush, and her lovely eyes were sparkling. "Coffee for my erstwhile lord and master. No sugar, no cream—you see, I've remembered."

"And what are you doing to the dentist, Clara?"

"Taking his money—why?"

"Listen—"

"No lecture, Danny. He began it, this poor fool did. Danny, isn't it comical how a small-town squirt such as Ken Jones is always convinced he knows all the answers and can always wow all the ladies?"

"Dawn March happened to be in love with him."

"Florence Nightingale? Well, then, Danny, pin a medal on me. Florence Nightingale will never awaken as a wife to the nasty fact that she's married to a lemon. Incidentally, I think she hates me."

"Why shouldn't she? You've spoiled several things for her. She deserved a better break."

"We all deserve breaks we're never given, didn't your mother ever tell you? Even I, Danny. I shall tell you a touching little story. I shall tell you of a girl, a very beautiful girl, who one day went to Princeton to see a football game. This girl was excited. There were women in furs, wearing chrysanthemums, there were happy college guys, and there was greensward under a perfect autumn sky. And that, Danny, was the beginning of a love story."

"I loved you."

"Yes, Danny."

"It would have worked."

"No, Danny."

"Why not?"

"Because you couldn't let it work. You couldn't be a husband to the girl after the excitement had worn off because you were living for you, Danny, not for me. Take a job with your father? Sure. But keep that job, nuts! Ho, for the bohemian existence. And the apartments grew smaller, became drearier, became colder. And so the girl woke up to the nasty fact that she was married to a lemon. And there were the dollars . . . waiting . . . waiting . . . and the marriage died."

He swallowed down a lump that had formed in his throat. He raised the coffee cup to his lips, and sipped. It was good strong coffee, and he sipped again.

"Anyway," Clara Royce said, "the fellow Florence Nightingale should marry is the big real estate lug. He's quite a guy, you know. I think he's the only person in the area who isn't interested in getting in on the land boom."

"Yup," Dan conceded, "Wes is quite a guy. He helped me out at a darned tough time."

"Go back to New York, Danny."

His eyes narrowed.

"I mean it," she said urgently, "for your own good. A time comes, Danny, when you become too attached to even a dismal hole, you even become happy in your hole, and what happens? The years go by and it's suddenly too late to climb out of the hole. Then all your life you're poor, alone and lonely, and—"

"Did you tell my father I was living here?"

"Yes."

"Why?"

Clara shrugged prettily. "Call it a remnant of love, Danny, I don't know. I'm told a woman never quite forgets her first husband. Perhaps that's true. You love the first one with such fierce ardor and with such breathless wonder and with—"

"The truth is," Danny shouted, "that you do still love me, and that you're here because of that. Now you've got the swag, and now you want the thing you left. Isn't that it?"

The eyes of Clara Royce danced, but her lips were thin and very still.

Dan Colby stood up, roaring with laughter. He sputtered: "What a mess you are, my dear ex-wife. I think you sold out for nothing."

She shook her head. Very softly, and with pity in her tones, she said: "You always did love me, Danny, as an emotionally immature man loves a creature of his most sentimental dreams. The creature must not be a mortal woman, with her foibles and frailties, heaven forfend. She must stand in all her pristine purity on a pedestal, and she must always stand there until the lord and master has time for her. Poor Danny. Well, drink your coffee, there's a dear."

He strode to the door, opened it dramatically. "Get going, Clara."

She rose languidly. "You are becoming attached to your hole, aren't you?"

The foghorn blew, fell silent, blew again. The fog had reached the dump and was spilling over the chain link fence and rolling on toward Clara's parked car.

"Danny?"

"Clara?"

"Your father did the thing he thought was best. You may disagree that his methods were what they should have been, but you must agree his motives were all right. You don't hurt him, either, living here as you do. You hurt yourself, and for no good reason. There. I've said all I intend to say."

"Are you being paid to say it?"

Clara shrugged and walked out. She drove away, and then all that Danny could see in the world was that rolling fog, and all he could hear in the world was the dismal, monotonous, somewhat eerie foghorn.

Chapter XV

Toward the end of July, just as she was getting ready to bake Wes a birthday cake, Dawn heard a ring of the doorbell. When she opened the door she didn't quite gape, but apparently she looked so surprised she was comical. Mrs. Clara Royce laughed. Mrs. Clara Royce said, "Oh, I'm real all right, Miss March. May I have a chat with you?"

"Well—I am busy—a cake, you know—anyway, Mrs. Royce—"

"Thank you, Miss March." And with her customary poise, her languid grace, Mrs. Clara Royce stepped in and found her own way into the living-room. The living-room interested her as it interested all people. She studied the model ships on the mantelshelf of the fireplace, she studied the paintings on the walls, the big globe map of the world in a corner, and shook her lovely black head. "You almost have a home here, don't you? Have you noticed, Miss March, that most people live in houses, not homes?"

Dawn hurried back to the kitchen to pop the cake into the oven. She was quite upset. Now why hadn't the woman given her a fair warning? Why had the woman come along to catch her in such grubby clothes as these?

Mrs. Royce invaded the kitchen. She looked at the bowls, the electric beater, and sniffed the air. "I do approve of domesticity," she announced. "You're an unusual girl, Miss March, aren't you? You do your duty to your community, and you do your duty to yourself as a woman. I marvel that some man hasn't snatched you long before this."

Dawn thought gloomily that no man ever would. Was she growing younger or prettier? Clearly not! True, she could marry Wes. But what did she have now to bring to Wes? A headful of shattered dreams, an older body, a somewhat weary and disillusioned mind.

"What did you wish," she asked quietly. "I think it is quite apparent, Mrs. Royce, that you wish something."

107

Clara Royce sat down, dressed in a sport skirt and a rather sheer striped blouse. Although it was a scorcher in Port West, she looked quite cool and comfortable, and contented with the weather, herself, and life. "Now you must not become cynical," she chided. "It isn't like you, Miss March. And don't grimace, please, because you know I speak the truth. There, that is the advantage I have over you. I have seen enough to know the truth when I see it. Do you know where Dan Colby is?"

"Dan Colby?"

"Your erstwhile patient at the community dump. He left. I had arranged to present him to an important television producer today, but when I went to his place I discovered he'd packed his clothes and scooted off."

Dawn blinked. "But why would he want to do that?"

"He's cross with me, of course. You see, Miss March, Dan Colby and I—well, actually we're old friends. And I made the mistake of telling his father where Danny could be found, and I think Danny became angry."

Dawn, interested, forgot she was cross with the woman. "There," she said excitedly, "I knew you hadn't come to him that evening to buy a painting!"

"Actually, I would like to own his paintings. Call it a sentimental whim. No matter. Knowing Danny, I'm worried about him. Where would he go without money, and how would he live?"

Dawn had an inspiration and hurried to the 'phone. She caught Wes at his office, and the big fellow was hugely pleased. "Can't wait to see me, eh? Well, that's how it should be, Dawn. Just keep on looking at me as a normal woman looks at a normal man and maybe you'll develop that natural yearning for—"

"Will you be quiet? Dan Colby's flown the coop!"

"Huh?"

"Mrs. Royce is here with me now. And she says that Dan Colby scooted with all his clothes and things."

"Now there's something," Wes conceded. "I thought nothing and no one would ever blast him out of that shack. Look, I'll be right over."

There was an interesting chat when Wes arrived. It occurred out on the front lawn of the March place where people could occasionally get a breath of fresh sea air. In the torrid heat the sky was a pale blue and all the trees and flowers stood motionless and somewhat limply.

"Well, Clara," Wes began the chat, "what did you do to Dan?"

"I?"

"Clara, Dan and I became pretty good friends. I know a lot about Dan's affairs."

"I see."

Dawn wished that she saw. Why was Wes so grim; why was Clara Royce so distraught?

A mockingbird provided a momentary distraction. The bird flew down from one of the magnolia trees to the bird bath standing in the fuchsia garden close to the front of the yellow cement-block house. The bird took a quick drink, then flew back to the tree.

"Poor guy," Wes said, "he must've been thirsty to invade a yard filled with people. You know, folks, this will probably be the hottest day in our short but glorious history."

Dawn understood what he was trying to do, and she loved him for it, and pitched in with her own two cents. "Anyone want some iced tea? And what about sitting down in the shade of the patio?"

Clara Royce gestured irritably. "I did nothing to Danny Colby, Mr. Overton. If you know as much about his affairs as you say, you know it was one of those minor tragedies you hear about every day. Say we were too young and foolish, or in too much of a hurry to live. No matter."

"But it does matter, I'm afraid. He still loves you, Clara. And call me Wes."

"Shall we say, Wes, that he loves me up to a point?"

Bewildered, Dawn went over to the trunk of one of the magnolia trees and sat down in the deep pool of shade. She studied the beautiful woman standing in the torrid glare of the sun. So this was the thing that had brought her to Port West? Then what about her pursuit of Ken? It didn't make sense! How could she possibly prefer Dan Colby to Ken Jones? Dan Colby was basically a self-centered weakling, a nice enough person, really, but certainly not a man for any woman to love. Why, it was downright fantastic!

Big Wes took a cigarette from a pack and lighted up. Dressed in gabardine slacks and a pale grey seersucker sport-shirt, his face flushed in the heat, his expression thoughtful, he had the air of a man becoming involved in complications he didn't particularly like.

"Dan Colby's an adult," he finally said. "I imagine he knows what he's doing. Did he have a battle with you?"

"A silly quarrel. Not with me, however. With himself, I suspect. I think you know where he went, Wes."

"I have an idea. There's a cheap hotel in Los Angeles that he likes. He's been there before to get a change of scene. By the way, I think you ought to return some money to Dr. March."

The blue eyes widened.

Then, without another word, Mrs. Clara Royce went to her car and drove off.

Wes just stood there grinning. He didn't move or speak until the mockingbird flew down once more to take another drink at the bird bath. "Too hot for me," he finally muttered. "Let's go to the beach or something."

Dawn shook her head. "Things to do here. How did my father's money get into this business?"

"Well, I expect to be his son-in-law some day. I don't want to have to support him in his old age."

Dawn flushed, averted her eyes.

"Anyway," Wes growled, "I dislike seeing a nice old guy cheated. He's being cheated, all right. I've done some snooping around. No important person in town has been approached by anyone even remotely interested in establishing a factory of any kind in our fair city. I think the lovely Mrs. Royce is being clever."

"But wasn't there talk that—"

"The Klaus organization?"

"According to Pop, the Hans Klaus organization is supposed to be interested."

"Suppose, Dawn, that Mrs. Royce had made a deal of some kind to get an expression of interest from them? Maybe they're involved in all this option buying that's going on. It would be slick. Big company expresses an interest in a certain tract of land. Grabs options. People become excited, want to be in on the kill when land values rise. Options sold at huge profits, big money made."

"But an organization that large!"

"Organizations usually become large because they know how to make money."

110

"But that would be dishonest!"

"How? All they're professing is an interest in a certain tract of land. And they would be interested, if not in the way people suppose."

But Dawn couldn't quite accept that. "I don't think you've hit it, Wes. By the way, where is Dan staying in Los Angeles?"

"Uh-uh."

"Wes!"

He joined her under the magnolia. "Your dogooding nature is beginning to show, Dawn. I prefer you as you are now, just a beautiful woman sitting under a tree with me."

"But you heard what she said! She wants to introduce him to a television producer! Wes, don't you see—if he could get some publicity he might pick up a few commissions. Wes, you can't cheat him of that chance, hang it."

"Do you know who he is, Dawn?"

"Oh, it's obvious that he has a background. He had a quarrel with his father, as I recall it, and—"

"His father is Thomas Colby, Dawn, of the Colby Steel Corporation."

"You're joking!"

"And the quarrel, Dawn, involved Clara Royce—only she was Clara Colby then. The father bought her off, thinking he was sparing his son a lifetime of grief. And I'd say the father was right, at that."

"Wes, that's fantastic!"

"Here in Port West, sure. Compared to Mr. Colby, even our big shots are little shots. Social position, all that, means very little here. Take the Pattons. It didn't mean a toot to them that Grey married one of our Oxton telephone operators. But in New York, and if you're up there on top of the social heap—well, apparently it did make a difference to Mr. Colby. Anyway Clara Colby skipped out, for a fee. Dan had a battle with his father, and ended up bumming his way across the country. All that was five years ago, and Clara has been married twice since then, and Dan—well, he tended to go to pot. Then he learned she was in southern California, and he got into touch with her and she was amused. Then he came here, and she came here because—well, I still think it had something to do with a darned clever scheme."

"And Ken?"

The reddish-brown eyes met hers squarely. "The only reason I didn't tell Mrs. Royce exactly what I thought of her is that I'm glad she took an interest in Ken. Look, you finally woke up. You saw him for what he is, a guy who'd junk you like that if he thought he could do better elsewhere. And don't tell me he shouldn't be blamed. He's trying to get in on this kill with her, and you know it."

But Dawn couldn't see it in quite that way. She could concede now that Ken's interest in her had been a rather mild one at best. Clearly, a man in love would not have been able to junk her so easily and readily. But she couldn't accept the suggestion that Ken Jones was the sort of man to whom success was all-important. He was ambitious, certainly, but not so ambitious he'd become involved in a slick scheme to mulct even his friends of their savings.

"We're digressing," she said flatly. "I still want to see Dan. And it's too bad, isn't it, that I happen to like people well enough to want to help them when I can. I'm sorry I'm not a Mrs. Clara Royce. Would it please you to see me degenerate into another Mrs. Clara Royce?"

His brow furrowed. "There's a happy medium, Dawn."

"To set the record straight, Wes, you can't be a good nurse or doctor if you don't like people. It's difficult work, and often it's unpleasant work. But it's work you have to do, if you like people, because certainly someone has to do the work. It isn't, anyway, as if I were a person with a one-track mind. I'm interested in many things, even in marrying, having a home—all that."

"Just not interested in marrying me?"

Dawn shrugged. "How can I answer that now? I've always been fond of you. Until I met Ken I even thought that one day I'd marry you. Then I did meet Ken, and things changed. Who knows—maybe I craved for the unknown he seemed to represent. Or maybe, because I didn't know him as well as I knew you, he seemed more exciting, glamorous—anyway, we're still digressing. I want Dan's address, if you have it."

"What do you expect to do?"

"Talk to him. If his father is so important, then his life here never made sense. I think it's foolish to throw big things away, to fiddle around in a dump, say, when you can accomplish truly important things."

"He's been told all that."

Dawn didn't care. She persisted until Wes finally gave her the address. She then went upstairs to her mother's room, told her mother to watch the cake in the oven, and dressed for a quickie trip to Los Angeles. In Los Angeles she discovered that the cheap hotel was actually a badly run-down rooming house for men; and the old fellow who greeted her at the grimy desk in the small lobby looked scandalized to see her even standing there. "Girlie," he snapped, "ain't you got better sense than t' bother with our bums here? You scoot home where you belong."

"Mr. Dan Colby, please."

"Ain't in."

"I'll wait."

He grumbled, but finally shuffled over to a panel of push-buttons on the wall. He pressed a button, and presently Dan came down the lobby stairs. For a bum, he looked incredibly clean, neat, well-dressed, and even the old sourpuss behind the desk looked surprised. "Son," he asked, "if you can dress like that what are you doin' livin' here?"

Dan looked at Dawn in her tan gabardine suit. His lips quirked, his blue eyes twinkled. "A delightful surprise, Miss March. Merely a coincidence, I presume?"

Dawn led him out to her car.

"Why did Wes tell you where I am, Miss March?"

"I asked him to. Dan, this is none of my business, but where does it all end? If you ever had a point, you've made it. But your father has made his, too. Or are you still in love with your ex-wife?"

"He shouldn't have told you that."

"Mrs. Royce is worried, Dan. Another thing—she'd arranged for you to meet a television producer this afternoon. It might have done you some good."

"She's an odd woman, Miss March."

"An odd woman?"

"I shouldn't still be in love with her. She represents everything I dislike in people. She's greedy, self-centered, as hard as iron, and—"

"Would it make a difference, Dan, if I were to tell you that your father really does need you? He isn't entirely well."

He stared.

"Mom told me about it just before I came here, Dan. I think you ought to return to New York."

"Why did he interfere? I'd have outgrown it!"

"But you didn't, Dan, did you? I have money for the ticket, if you're broke."

He inhaled deeply. Then Dan Colby began to talk, and that was when Dawn agreed, in her heart, that Dan's father had used the wrong tactics.

She was thoughtful during the long drive back to Port West. She suddenly understood why Wes and Dan had hit it off from the very beginning. They were very much alike, those two. When they fell in love, they fell in love for good.

Chapter XVI

NELLIE GRAND LISTENED, HER HANDS FOLDED ON HER spanking new walnut desk. When Dawn had finished talking, Nellie's head made a quick bob forward, and then Nellie chuckled. "I find it interesting," Nellie said, "to see how often life arranges the punishment to fit the crime. Have you told Ken Jones?"

"No, ma'am."

"Don't. It will be a service to humanity the day he loses his shirt. He'll then settle down to his business, as a good dentist should."

"The trouble with that, though, is the fact that others will lose out if he does. I was talking to Sammy Berman this morning. He tells me that Mrs. Royce has unloaded a number of options and that people are growing more interested every day."

The little woman heaved a sigh. "That would be unfortunate," she agreed. "Still, what can you actually prove? As I see it, Dan Colby may have told you the truth, but the truth will be difficult to prove."

"I could write the Klaus organization."

"If they're involved, however . . ."

Dawn nodded. There was the rub. She had it all now, but none of it could be used. And so the clever scheme that had been hatched by the clever mind of Mrs. Clara Royce would work. In the end, Mrs. Royce would leave the Port West-Oxton community fifty or sixty thousand dollars richer. And the poor, gullible idiots she left behind her?

"It isn't right," she said. "Nellie, it isn't right."

"Many things aren't right. By the way, I have been thinking it is time you were transferred back to your old territory. I disliked the idea of assigning you to a territory so close to your home. Nurses do an excellent job, I find, when they approach their work in a thoroughly objective fashion. Will it be agreeable if I make the transfer effective on the 15th of August?"

Dawn didn't care. She grinned as she rose. "Suit yourself, Nellie. I'm the willing Dobbin, as always."

"Or perhaps it's time you were given a tour of duty here in administration. I may as well tell you, March, that I think you have good possibilities. You do have a tendency to become emotional, but in time you'll curb that tendency, I'm sure."

Dawn stopped short, halfway to the door. "Now that isn't fair, Nellie. You know I prefer field duty."

"We all have preferences, March. Unfortunately, we are obligated to serve where we are required. That will be all."

"But—"

Dawn broke off there, knowing that when Nellie Grand had made a decision she couldn't be talked into changing her mind. In an angry frame of mind, she drove back to Port West.

She found Hattie waiting in the living-room, and Hattie looked cross, worried, tired. "I wondered if you'd ever come back home." Hattie said. "I'd like to talk to you."

And this, too, Dawn thought, was a problem. The perky blonde had become interested in Dan Colby. Not too interested, she hoped but perhaps interested enough to feel hurt, confused, upset. "Hi." She smiled. "Let's take the evening off and go to Los Angeles for dinner."

"Where is he, Dawn?"

"Where's who?"

"Dan Colby."

"New York."

Hattie started. Yes, there it was on her face, the proof that she'd become interested enough to feel hurt, confused, upset.

"But why? I mean, he was doing such good work right here."

"Because the time had come for him to stop feeling sorry for himself. Can you take a shock, Hattie? Dan Colby and Mrs. Royce were married once upon a time."

The gray eyes bugged. The face of Harriette Jones went pale.

"He still loves her, Hattie, and will probably always love her. I learned all that when I saw him in Los Angeles last week. Sorry, but that's how it is."

"You lie!"

Dawn sat down on the couch. She felt hot, tired, and wanted to go upstairs and have a long, cooling, bracing shower. But this was a kid in emotional trouble, and she certainly owed it to Hattie to say and do what she could.

116

"Dan would marry her again tomorrow if he could, Hattie. He probably will, one day, because I think that Clara Royce, in her way, still loves him. It's a good thing you didn't become interested in him, isn't it?"

"Interested?" Hattie clutched at it, forced a laugh. "Now you are being silly. Why, to me he was just a poor fellow who needed someone to talk to, someone to take an interest in him."

"Strange, isn't it? Yet people think that life in a small town is dull. Why, right there in our community dump was the son of a steel corporation executive. And the lovely Clara Royce, who was so busy buying up land and talking big business deals, was his ex-wife and a thief, and a—"

"Thief?"

"Hattie, you may as well know that Ken was taken for the well-known buggy-ride. Sorry, but no factory will be established over there near the dump. Mrs. Royce was simply busy making money."

Hattie half rose, then sank back to her chair weakly. "But Ken's invested every penny we had! He—why, he even borrowed some money from the bank."

Dawn said nothing, because there seemed so little to say. After Hattie had left, she went upstairs and took that long, cool, bracing shower, then put on a cotton dress and drove back to Oxton to have dinner with Sammy Berman. The long lean redheaded lawyer greeted her outside the restaurant with a big grin. "Too bad this couldn't be at the house, Dawn. Well, it looks pretty good. I don't say that Dover will be declared not guilty, but I think I created a large doubt in the minds of the jury. You'd better grab your chow in a hurry. I've left word I can be reached here if the jury announces that it's made a decision."

A quiver of excitement ran through Dawn's stomach. She hustled into the restaurant and ordered a salad, and over the salad she asked: "Convinced that he's innocent, Sammy?"

"Yup."

"But who embezzled the money?"

"Who knows? Dover panicked, I do know that. He was responsible for the money, and he knew darned well that it would be hung on him, so he bought that plane ticket. Panic is a queer thing. Care to hear something about panic?"

"Well?"

117

"Mrs. Clara Royce is feeling panicky. It seems that she received an official communication from the Hans Klaus organization to the effect that it is no longer interested in a certain tract of land. Mrs. Royce is stuck with options she doesn't want to pick up. But, unfortunately, she's paid quite a bit for those options, and it would seem that the few sales she's made won't begin to compensate her for the losses she'll incur when the news is made public."

Dawn whistled; she couldn't help it.

Sammy Berman nodded. "The only reason I'm telling you this is that the news will be made public—in fact, it already has been made public. Did you see the headlines in the papers?"

And there it was, Dawn thought.

"The Klaus organization, unfortunately for Mrs. Royce, also sent a copy of their letter to our newspapers. I think she's a bit upset. How can anyone say she was dishonest when the organization did admit it had been interested in that land? Anyway, she's given me a retainer to defend her against lawsuits."

Exit Mrs. Royce, Dawn thought. She smiled tightly.

"Do you know something, Sammy? I don't think I've ever disliked a person as intensely as I dislike Mrs. Clara Royce. She's a spoiler. She spoiled her life, Dan's life, Ken's life, my life, and probably the lives of a lot of people around here who were sold something not worth a tenth of the asking price. How can people like her exist?"

He cleared his throat, but before he could answer the question their waitress came over with the news that the jury was prepared to announce its decision. Dawn loped out into the evening with Sammy and invited herself to go to the courtroom with him. She was all pins and needles with excitement when she stepped into the courtroom, but Sammy looked relaxed and even bored. She felt annoyed with him. "You could be human, you know. You could be as excited and worried as I."

"I go through this fifteen or twenty times a year. I think he'll be declared not guilty. Usually a decision of guilty is made quickly. But I could be wrong."

The judge appeared at his bench at the forward end of the courtroom. Mr. Dover was brought in, looking pale and shrunken, and then the jury filed into the jury box. The foreman of the jury stood up, cleared his throat, and in reply to the judge's question announced that the jury had reached a verdict and that the verdict was "Not guilty."

The district attorney jumped hotly to his feet. "What did you want," he roared, "a picture of this man opening that safe?"

Dawn hustled up front to the pale and shrunken man sitting as if stunned in the prisoner's box. "Hi." She grinned. "Long time no see, Mr. Dover."

He studied her happy, pretty face. He smiled faintly. "Oh, it's Miss March, isn't it? Delighted to see you, Miss March. How are your father and mother?"

"Quite well, sir. Your wife, incidentally, has taken all this very well."

"Why not, Miss March? She was aware the charge was ridiculous."

He stood up and looked inquiringly at the judge. The judge nodded, the guards stepped away, and Mr. Dover stepped out of the prisoner's box. He went over to Sammy Berman and pumped that doughty individual's hand, and then he turned and with quickening steps headed toward the door at the rear of the courtroom.

Sammy grinned. "Would you say he's anxious to see his wife?"

"I'd say so. Sammy, you ought to feel proud of yourself."

But there was someone who disagreed. The district attorney came over to them grimly. He ignored Dawn. He looked up at the redhead's face and barked: "It was cheap trickery, Berman. Who else could have done it?"

"I wouldn't know. But it wasn't trickery. The people who testified he was in the Mexican quarter that night were honest people. You tried to shake them, but you couldn't. And do you know why you couldn't? Because they were telling the truth. Sure, you were gunning for a conviction. So you were very happy to grab the obvious suspect and—"

"Are you insinuating I'd send an innocent man to jail?"

"Not knowingly. But I do think you did a poor job of preparing your case."

The district attorney turned away hotly. "Well, you haven't heard the last of this, Berman. That was a guilty man who was freed. I'll bet my last dollar on it."

They went back into the evening, and the fresh air was

119

good and so were the stars beginning to gleam in the August sky. Sammy let his breath out and shook his head. "A rough case, Dawn. Please don't telephone me again when you have a lame duck in trouble. Just forget the Bermans are alive."

"As you wish."

"Dawn, I put in almost a solid month of work. I talked to everyone in the bank, I talked to just about everyone in the Mexican quarter. I'm bushed."

"But you should feel proud of yourself, Sammy."

"Blah."

But he was, Dawn knew, and she chuckled and relaxed in the car while he drove her home. She was very happy to find Wes sitting in her living-room, and she promptly proceeded to do some crowing. "So it's wrong to be dedicated to humanity, is it? Well, Mr. Dover's out of the clink. And the only reason justice was done is that a couple of stupid do-gooders weren't inclined to forget someone in trouble."

"Huh?"

Dawn sat down, grinning. "Care to hear something else, Wes? The whole thing's beginning to work out. The Klaus organization isn't interested in that land, and—"

"Read about it in the paper. You had a visitor."

"Oh?"

"Ken Jones. It seems that Clara Royce has taken off to parts unknown." Wes laughed shortly, but not with satisfaction. "I felt sorry for the guy. He's beginning to understand he was played for a sucker."

Dawn felt sorry for Ken, too, and that astonished her. There'd been so many moments of bitterness, so many moments when she'd actually hoped something like this would happen to the fellow who'd been so intent upon great success.

The red-brown eyes swung to her. "I suppose you'll see him, Dawn?"

"Of course."

"And he'll tell you it was one of those things—that actually he'd loved you all along, that he'd always intended to marry you when he could support you in the style to which you'd grown accustomed."

"I suppose so."

"I won't, Dawn. You know where I live, what I do, how you'll probably always live if you marry me. I want it, sure.

120

But I won't try to sell you a bill of goods. I won't even make a final pitch now. You know how I've always felt."

Dawn nodded, and Wes just got up and left.

A split-second after the front door had closed her father stepped out into the hall. He was coatless, tieless, and he looked testy and flustered, as he always did when he was engaged in an important task of writing. "How did Dover make out?" he asked.

"Not guilty."

"It had to be that way. I know Dover. The man is as honest as they make them. What was Sammy Berman's fee?"

"No fee."

"That's like Sammy. I think I'll propose his name when we have our county elections. He ought to be our district attorney. Ought to be a judge some day, too. That boy is all heart. Our jurists should be all heart. You look well."

"What do you want, Pop?"

Her dancing brown eyes were somewhat roguish, and it suddenly occurred to him that this was the old Dawn March, the girl who could josh and be joshed, the girl who'd always gotten a big bang out of the experience of just living.

"Well," he joshed back, "your mother has changed her mind. She doesn't like her so-called formal Japanese garden. You could eliminate that confounded ornamental pool, for one thing. I stepped into it the other night. A miserable puddle of water, three inches deep, good only for attracting mosquitoes."

"Writing a lecture, Pop?"

"Well, I'm taking my vacation in September. In October I'll deliver a series of lectures. So I'm preparing the lectures now. Care to read my latest masterpiece?"

"Sure."

He smiled happily.

He led her into his office and gestured at his desk. "Read them all," he invited her. "Ken Jones telephoned, incidentally. He also paid us a visit. And Mrs. Royce telephoned you from New York."

"From where?"

"To tell you, Dawn, that Ken Jones was aware the Klaus interest in Port West wasn't genuine."

Dawn's mouth clicked shut. Contempt flared in her big brown eyes. . . .

121

Y ES, HATTIE ADMITTED, IT WAS TRUE. ONE THING HAD led to another, and the inevitable had happened. A fine state of affairs, wasn't it? And wouldn't Dawn just love to buy the house, the dental office, and Ken's business?

Dawn said no. She smiled and gave the troubled blonde head a pat. "It'll be all right," she soothed. "He's a good dentist, you know. He'll make it all back, and then some."

"In Port West?"

"Why not?"

"Here, where everyone knows the fool he was, and what he tried to do?"

"He knew all about it, then?"

Hattie sat down on the sand. She looked moodily off toward the horizon. "Not everything," she conceded. "But he suspected most of it, and he certainly shouldn't have become involved."

"But if he'd made money, you see, everyone would have called him bright. And he didn't miss by much, you know. She made just one mistake. If she'd not been responsible for his father's visit . . ."

Hattie laughed bitterly. It was obvious that she wasn't at all inclined to make excuses for her brother or to hear anyone else imply that he wasn't quite the greedy idiot she'd said he was. "I've told him I'm leaving, Dawn. It has to be. Everyone was kind to us. We came here as strangers, and within six months—well, he tried to cheat people who'd been kind to us, and that's unforgivable. I won't live here now, period."

"Where will you live?"

Hattie's chin came up. "New York, maybe. I've always wanted to live in New York."

Dawn began to understand. She didn't know what to say, so, wisely, she said nothing. She studied the ocean before them. This ocean, she recalled, had come to mean much to Daniel Colby. He'd learned its ways, he'd learned something

122

of its creatures. So his experience here had been beneficial, and now that he'd left the hole possibly he'd be all right. But would he be all right for Hattie?

"Yes," Hattie said breathlessly, "I love him. I did the first time we met. And I won't let her hurt him again."

"I see."

"There's too much hurt, Dawn. There's so much taking, so little giving. There's so much cynicism, so little faith in people, in life . . . I wish he'd not left so soon."

"His father needed him, and he needed his father. I hope you know what you're doing, however. It may be rough in New York. And how will you live?"

"Take a job. If he won't see me, then that will have to be that. But I intend to go there just the same."

"Need any money?"

"I have enough. Ken was always nice about that. He never tried to get the three thousand dollars our father left me. I don't suppose he's all greed, at that."

"Few people are ever wholly good or wholly bad, you goop. My father's called good, and heaven knows that he is. Still, he does like to have his own way. Or consider Ken. Sure, he wanted money, money in gobs. But he always kept the appointments he had at the free dental clinics, didn't he?"

"I often wondered why."

"Because he isn't all bad, that's why. When do you expect to leave?"

"September 1st. Ken's pretty furious. He feels that I'm letting him down just when he needs me most. But I just can't see it that way. I argued, he wouldn't listen. I pleaded, he just laughed. What can I do for him now? Can I put his self-respect back together for him? It's just a mess, that's all."

Inwardly, Dawn agreed. She smiled with a practiced show of amusement, however. "Oh, I doubt it, Hattie. Anyway, we'll see. You'll see me a lot before you leave, won't you?"

The gray eyes met hers, and there were tears in them, and Hattie came dangerously close to blubbering. "Will you tell me why men have to be such fools? He had something wonderful. All he had to do was reach out and take it. Now?"

Yes, Dawn thought, that was a major question, too. Now the summer storm was almost over. And what had the storm left in its aftermath? A great many people angry, and several

123

people just about broke. What about them, and what about herself?

"I don't suppose you could see him?" Hattie asked. "I mean, just to talk to him, to tell him things aren't quite as bad as they really are?"

Dawn looked over her shoulder at the green house on Maricopa Street. She didn't particularly want to enter that house, nor did she particularly want to see Ken. Still, who was she to say no when someone needed help? Nellie would be scandalized if she were to refuse.

She stood up, brushed the sand from her skirt. "Why don't you just sit here for a few minutes, Hattie? It's a beautiful view, isn't it?"

"Dan loved it. I think he loved Port West."

Dawn didn't disillusion her, but turned and began the walk to the green house in Maricopa Street.

She opened the gate and stepped into the yard. She rang the doorbell, and when he opened the door she trotted out her professional smile. "Hi, Ken," she said, "long time no see."

"Oh, it's you? Well, what a pleasant surprise. Do come in, Dawn, won't you?"

Dawn stepped into the little vestibule and waited for him to close the front door. He gestured her into his small office on the left, and she took a chair beside his small metal desk. The papers lying strewn across the desk told her the whole dismal story, and she sighed.

Ken shrugged. "Thirty acres of land represented by those papers. Options to buy them. Do you know what I can do with those options?"

"Eat them, I imagine."

"Very amusing, and I didn't know you could gloat."

"I can. In all ways, Ken, I'm a normal human being. I can love and be happy, or I can fall out of love and be sad. What do you expect people to do—say they're sorry?"

He scowled and sat down. "No, that part of it is all right. The thing that irks most is that I was actually growing fond of her. It wasn't my intention, I assure you. At one time I excused my behavior by thinking it was all being done for you. Then . . . she's a strange girl, Dawn."

"Not strange. Just a girl."

"What's wrong with her, Dawn?"

124

"Nothing, really. She simply knew what she wanted and went after it. I doubt her standards were high, so she could do the things she did with little remorse or compunction. To her, I think, the ends do justify the means. Wes wants me to marry him."

"You should."

"I know."

"Candidly, Dawn, you're too dull for me. I don't mean that to sound the way it does. It's simply that Clara Royce stimulated me, made life pleasant. I'm afraid I wasn't created to function as a small-town dentist."

"What were you created to do, Ken?"

"Make money."

She looked down at the littered desk top.

Ken laughed softly. "Yes, the evidence would seem to refute that, wouldn't it? But I don't know Consider the position of the Hans Klaus organization, Dawn. I have knowledge that would embarrass them. I think it would be worth their while to reimburse me for the losses I incurred. Then I'll sell out, find another place and begin again. It isn't the end of the road—one reversal. Think of all the successful men who had to start over and over a dozen times before they made good. Would that life appeal to you?"

It occurred to Dawn that in some way he'd contrived to get control of this chat, and the knowledge startled her. She met his eyes four-square. "You know it wouldn't."

"Then why hate me, Dawn? Why even feel bitter? Shall I tell you something? There was much about me that you never knew for the simple reason that I knew you'd let it all die there. And at that time . . . well, it's quite easy to love you, Dawn. You take yourself a bit too seriously, and there are times when your devotion to mankind becomes a bit— well, sticky. On the other hand, you are capable of astonishing kindnesses, and your principles do mean a great deal to you, and that does make you, I'm afraid, a woman with character. It's always easy to love a woman with character who also happens to be quite beautiful."

"But you're not the sort to settle down, is that it?"

"Not with Clara Royce loose in the world," he said simply. He stood up, his gray eyes sparkling, a pink tinge of excitement in his cheeks. "Do you know what I've been thinking,

125

Dawn? I've been thinking that Clara and I would make a good team."

Dawn shook her head, not laughing at this because it struck her as being tragic. "No, Ken. You forget two important things. First, she had a hundred thousand in cash to start with—the fee she received for breaking up her marriage to Dan. Second, she does have a genius, an evil genius, if you will, for seeing opportunities and for using her beauty and money to exploit those opportunities to the hilt. You? Well, you lack the money, you lack the genius. You're simply a dentist who lost your shirt because all you really have is a rather pathetic greed."

It stung. He drew a sharp breath and took an angry step toward her. But the door chimes rang, and he whirled and went out to the vestibule. It was the Lem Swink boy, with a telegram for Harriette Jones. Ken looked at the yellow envelope, then cupped his hands around his mouth and gave his sister a hail. Hattie came running, and when she saw the telegram her eyes rounded and her forehead crinkled. "But why should anyone want to send me a telegram, of all things?"

Dawn told her to open it, read it, and Hattie did. She gave a soft cry that could have signified pleasure or pain, and Ken snatched the telegram from her hand and did some reading of his own. He gave a short grunt, then turned and without a word just strode out of the house and slammed the front door shut behind him. It was Hattie's sudden chuckle that finally told Dawn the telegram had solved a few Jones problems. "From Dan," Hattie finally said. "He's made Clara Royce return the money she got from Ken. The check will be here in a couple of days. And he wanted to know if I ever intended to visit New York."

"I see." Dawn gave it some thought, then kissed the girl's flushed cheek and went outdoors again, in search of Ken. She spotted him standing on the beach, but he wasn't alone. Wes was ranged beside him and was doing some very earnest talking, and Wes didn't stop talking, either, when she joined them.

"The fact is," Wes said forcefully, "that this town needs you, Ken, just as it needs doctors and nurses. You know your job. And when you stick to the job you know, you're okay. And about getting ahead . . . who said you weren't getting ahead? You folks have been here just about a year and a

126

half. Look what you've accomplished! You have a home half paid for, you have money in the bank, you have all the business you can handle. And there'll be enough business, as time goes on, to justify building a bigger office and taking in one or two assistants. Lord, what do you expect to be, a millionaire?"

"Still—"

Big Wes interrupted with a laugh. "Sure, you have big ideas; who hasn't? Okay, take your money and lose it again. And go on doing that until it's too late for you to be anything but a bum. Will that make you happy?"

"He'll stay, and he'll be sensible, Wes."

They both turned to study Dawn's amused expression.

Dawn turned with a shrug. "He knows he was lucky, Wes. And he isn't so foolish as to think he'll be lucky again. And his so-called business ability? Pfui! He knows as well as we do that he fell like a fool into her trap and that he'd be a fool again, because you're either a fool or you're not, period. He'll be afraid to try a second time, don't you see?"

"Now look here," Ken snapped, "I don't have to take that even from you. Who are you to strut around pretending you're so intelligent, so all-wise? I was seeing her almost night after night for a month before you even woke up to the fact she was in town."

Dawn headed for her car, and didn't look back. He called other things after her, but she didn't really listen, thinking that the important thing had already been said.

She looked around as a hand touched her arm. She met the reddish-brown eyes of Wes, and grinned wryly. "He's pretty sore, isn't he?"

"The thing that hurts, I think, is the fact that he's actually receiving charity from that beautiful girl of his dreams who made such a fool of him. But you're right, Dawn. He knows he was a chump, and he knows he's lucky to have his money back. He'll be all right."

They reached the car, and Dawn got in behind the steering wheel. But she was in no hurry to leave. It was nice to be with Wes after all the stress and strain of her conversations with Hattie and Ken. It was nice to look at him and see not a problem but just a big guy who thought her the most beautiful, intelligent, kindest woman in all the wide, wide world.

"Let's take a drive?" she asked. "Let's have dinner in Los Angeles?"

"I'd have to change. What about letting me pick you up in an hour, say?"

Dawn nodded, smiled.

Wes sighed. "You shouldn't smile that way, Dawn. I don't know why, but that smile pleased me the first time I saw it. Would you like to hear another proposal?"

"Not today, Wes. And not tomorrow or next week or next month. But it would be nice to see you tomorrow and next week and next month. You're very nice, Wes. You're always there. And I like knowing you're there, and—"

Wes kissed her.

Dawn started to draw back, quite annoyed with him. At a time like this? Didn't he know she had much thinking to do?

And yet it was a pleasant kiss. It was a frank, unashamed declaration of love, and the love was an honest love, and it would always be there, too, just like big Wes Overton himself.

The thought pleased Dawn March.

The kiss made her tingle.

It would be very nice, she thought, to have a lifetime of such kisses!

Wes drew back, met her glowing brown eyes.

"You know what I think?" he asked.

"What?"

"That Nellie Grand will have to find another nurse within a year. To take your place, I mean."

"Listen, Wes . . ."

"I'll bet you a hundred dollars to fifty dollars, Dawn. Care to bet?"

She drew a deep breath. Then, to the delight of Wes Overton, she softly said: "No, I wouldn't want to bet against that, Wes. I never like to lose money, you see."